Charles Cros: Collected Monologues

Portrait of Cros & Coquelin

Charles Cros

COLLECTED

MONOLOGUES

Translated from the French by Doug Skinner

BLACK SCAT BOOKS
2018

CHARLES CROS:
COLLECTED MONOLOGUES
by Charles Cros
Translated from the French, with an introduction
& notes on the text by Doug Skinner

ISBN 13 978-1-7323506-2-5

Cover art & book design by Norman Conquest

Several of these texts first appeared in *Black Scat Review* #15

Second Printing

BLACK SCAT BOOKS
Sublime Art & Literature
BlackScatBooks.net — **BlackScatBooks.com**

CONTENTS

INTRODUCTION

CHARLES CROS (1842-1888) both puzzled and dazzled his contemporaries. He was thin and dark, with an unruly mop of kinky curls, and was often compared to a Hindu or Gypsy. He wrote delicate and personal poetry, contributed wild stories to Bohemian papers, and enlivened the extreme groups of Paris: the Zutistes, Hydropathes, and Vilains Bonhommes. Oddly enough, he was also an accomplished scientist, or, more properly, inventor, who experimented with color photography, synthetic gems, telegraphy, and other subjects; he famously invented the phonograph before Edison. He was brilliant and impractical, and died at 45, penniless and alcoholic. Along the way, he also pioneered a new theatrical genre, the comic monologue.

He came from a literary family. His grandfather, Antoine Cros, translated the Idylls of Theocritus; his father, Simon-Charles-Henri Cros, published a *Theory of Intellectual and Moral Man*. His brother Antoine-Hippolyte was a physician, wrote books of verse, medicine, and philosophy, and, not incidentally, was pretender to the ephemeral South American Kingdom of Araucanía and Patagonia; his brother César Isidore Henry was a sculptor, painter, ceramicist, and glazier, who also published research on ancient techniques of encaustic. A sister, Henriette, seems to have written no books; maybe some will turn up.

Émile-Hortensius-Charles Cros, the youngest of the four, was born in Fabrezan, in Aude, on October 13, 1842. He had little formal education, and was mostly taught by his father. Languages were apparently prized by the Cros family: by the time he was 17, Charles had some knowledge of Greek, Latin, Sanskrit, Hebrew, German, and Italian; he also found time for mathematics and music. At 18, he started teaching at the National Institute for the Deaf and Dumb (now the National Institute for Deaf Children) in Paris, only to be fired two years later for getting mixed up in a duel. He began to study medicine, but abandoned it in 1865.

He also became friendly with poets and artists. He started drinking heavily with Verlaine, and let Rimbaud stay in his studio; Rimbaud responded by destroying Cros's books and instruments.

Cros also met Nina de Villard, a fiery black-haired poet and pianist, who conducted a salon in Paris, attended by Villiers de L'Isle-Adam, Mallarmé, Verlaine, Anatole France, and many others. Charles and Nina eventually became lovers, and continued a stormy romance for some eight years. Naturally, Cros started writing poetry, much of it inspired by Nina. His publications included a long poem, *Le Fleuve* (*The River*), illustrated by Manet, and a collection of poetry and prose, *Le Coffret de Santal* (*The Sandalwood Box*). Along with his brothers and Rimbaud, among others, he founded the Zutistes, who amused themselves with filthy parodies of more respectable poets—especially François Coppée, who had rejected them from the prestigious anthology *Parnasse Contemporain*. (Coppée had also dismissed Baudelaire as "impossible," which he apparently considered a bad thing.) His poetry was prized by his colleagues; Verlaine called him "an irreproachable versifier, who brings his candid and perverse voice to every subject."

Somehow, his brain also found room for scientific research, bankrolled at times by the Duke of Chaulnes. He worked on synthetic gems, celestial photography, a radiometer, a photophone, a chromometer, a non-metallic battery (with Alphonse Allais), and a "musical stenographer" (with his brother Antoine). He made considerable progress in color photography, thanks in part to Manet, who loaned him paintings for the experiments. His scholarly publications included a *Principles of Celestial Mechanics*, and a plan to set up huge mirrors for communication with Mars.

He also invented the phonograph (which he called a *paléophone*) some eight and half months before Edison, who beat him to the patent office. For the details, see Alphonse Allais's article, "Charles Cros and Mr. Edison," later in this collection. As Allais notes, he was there.

After his inevitable rupture with Nina, he married a Danish woman, Mary Hjardemaal, and had two children, René and Guy-Charles (who later became a well-known poet himself). He became a regular at the Chat Noir, and contributed to *Scapin*, *Décadence*, and other papers. Alcohol was long a weakness, and his money problems became even worse after the Duke of Chaulnes died in 1881. Cros died August 9, 1888, at the age of 45.

The monologues form a unique part of his work, and often seem far ahead of their time. The first was *Le Hareng saur*, which I've translated here as "The Salt Herring," its usual name in English (although both "Kippered Herring" and "Red Herring" have their own tempting associations). According to a probably apocryphal story, Cros and some of his friends were staying with Verlaine's long-suffering mother during the war of 1870. Villiers de L'Isle-Adam passed out on a sofa, and Cros dangled a salt herring over his head. Inspiration followed. The first version was published in 1872, and then reworked for *The Sandalwood Box*. Cros was often called upon to recite it, which is how it came to the attention of Coquelin Cadet.

That was Ernest Coquelin, known as Coquelin Cadet (the younger) to distinguish him from his brother, Benoît-Constant, known as Coquelin Aîné (the older). Both were in the venerable Comédie-Française; the older brother was famous for his roles in Moliére and Rostand, particularly for creating the role of Cyrano, whereas the younger specialized in comedy, and had a taste for the boho circles of Montmartre. Coquelin Cadet described his discovery of "The Salt Herring" in a chapbook from 1881, *Le Monologue Moderne*:

"I recounted at this very table how the idea of transporting this new literary formula came to me on hearing 'The Salt Herring' one summer, at a dinner in Batignolles, at around four in the morning.

"Was it the milieu in which I found myself, the early hour, the gold from the east shining through the window, and the gold of the salt herring, that all mixed together in my mind? I saw then the dawn of the modern monologue, and no more curious impression has ever been granted me than that of hearing Cros recite, with the gravity of a man intoning Châteaubriand or Lamennais, his hilarious 'Salt Herring.' I did not suspect, at the time, that this little fish would grow so big, that it would be appreciated by the crowds that flock to music-halls, and that it would charm that ocean called Paris."

For Coquelin, the monologue was attractive for many reasons:

"For the actor, he produces his monologues alone. No prop, no direction, no 200,000 francs for the scenery for a spectacle, no stage manager to penalize you, no firemen—what savings! No arguments, unless you are so quarrelsome that you pick fights with yourself: the company is composed of a single actor: no jealousy! And you are your own manager.

"Your costume? A black suit."

Once prompted, Cros wrote more monologues, developing them into a fresh and personal genre. Actors previously had delivered excerpts from plays, recited verses, sung songs, or given lectures laced with witticisms. Cros created a gallery of fools and obsessives, often nattering away at high speed, blithely unconscious of their own failings. The language is decidedly in spoken syntax, with unfinished sentences, repetitions, hesitations, memory lapses and rapid shuttlings between the present and future tense. Several, deliberately and maliciously, bore the audience with trivia.

Monologues became popular, and soon every writer in Coquelin's circle was turning them out for him. As Coquelin said, "it is confected more easily than a tragedy, and is, in short, more fun."

Coquelin became famous for his monologues, and earned a lot of money from performing them. Unfortunately, Cros earned less from writing them. A squib from *Le Chat Noir* satirized the discrepancy (March 24, 1883):

"Charles Cros to Coquelin Cadet.—I still have an old monologue. Do you have an old frock coat? Your supplier, Charles Cros. Have pity, I'm dying of hunger."

The monologues were published, in the annual anthologies *Saynètes et Monologues* (*Sketches and Monologues*) and *Théâtre de Campagne* (*Country Theater*), both published by Tresse & Stock; some also sparked chapbooks. Here, too, Cros became exasperated with Coquelin, as in this 1878 letter to his publisher:

"My dear Madame Tresse,

"This is the exact text that must be published, and no other; I will not approve the final proof for anything else.

"Why the devil did you give Coquelin my proofs to correct? He's not the author, he's not my teacher in school. I alone am responsible for what I write; he can cut or add whatever he likes in performance, but do not consult him about the text that I sign.

"Pardon my harshness, but really, you were wrong to reinstitute a system that has already so justly irritated me, as you may recall.

"'The Rue Beaubourg Affair' no longer makes sense in the book, due to the cuts and changes made without my permission.

"In spite of everything, please accept my best wishes for you, and for Mademoiselle Tresse, my respectful salutations."

Eventually, the two colleagues fell out. As Madame Tresse's nephew, Pierre-Victor Stock, recounted in his memoirs:

"Somewhat disappointed to see his interpreter collect fees of five hundred francs, or a thousand francs, while he, the author, received nothing, he complained, and his relations with Cadet became strained. Taking Cros's cause in hand, I arrived at a secret arrangement by which, out of ten per cent of his fee, Coquelin Cadet would pay Cros the proportion due him, according to the number of his monologues performed in the course of the evening.

"This agreement was kept; but Cadet, who had been 'subjected' to it, performed no more new monologues by Cros, and gradually abandoned the repertory of his most appreciated author, for works by amateurs to whom he owed no royalties.

"Their interactions quickly became less frequent, and soon ceased completely: their collaboration was finished."

Cros then turned to another actor, Félix Galipaux. Galipaux was not only an actor, but a singer, violinist, and, unfortunately for Cros, perfectly capable of writing his own material. Among his curious activities were writing a play with Alphonse Allais (*Monsieur La Pudeur*, to which Paul Bonhomme also contributed) and portraying Raymond Roussel, thinly disguised as "Nointrel," in the theatrical adaptation of Roussel's *Locus Solus* in 1922.

Cros also wrote one monologue for Jeanne Samary, best remembered today as the model for several of Manet's paintings. Several were published with no indication of performer, which may mean that they were written specifically for publication.

Coquelin, however, was the primary performer of Cros's monologues. How, we may ask, did he perform them? Fortunately, he left detailed notes for posterity (that's us). In 1884, the two brothers wrote a book called *L'Art de dire le monologue* (*The Art of Speaking the Monologue*). Each set down his approach to the new and popular genre; Cadet annotated several pieces in his repertory, including two by Cros, "The Salt Herring" and "Obsession." Judging from his instructions, his style was unlike the usual Montmartre deadpan, but hyperactive, seasoned with plenty of mugging, physical gags, and vocal effects. He recorded several monologues in 1902 and 1903, for the Gramophone and Typewriter Company, whose records were distributed in Europe on the Zonophone label. In addition to morsels by Richepin, Thinet, Daudet, Bursault, Noel, and Nina de Villard, he recorded three by Cros: "The Salt Herring," "Obsession," and "The Capitalist." I've only been able to hear the last of these, and found it a clear and precise rendition, although abridged and compromised by the limitations of the technology, which, at that time, required the actor to stand still and bark into a cone. In 1906, Galipaux recorded his own version of "The Salt Herring," for the *Association Phonique de Grands Artistes*, which I was lucky enough to locate online. Galipaux's performance follows Coquelin's directions meticulously; perhaps by then they were mandatory.

As I mentioned earlier, Cros's technique in these pieces is rapid, spoken, and spontaneous. I've tried to keep my translations brisk, and have also kept Cros's expressive and idiosyncratic punctuation, studded with dashes, ellipses, commas, and semicolons, although I did replace guillemets with quotation marks. One of the monologues, "The Violin," is in verse. I retained the meter, but not the rhymes, which would have required too much overhauling. Please keep in mind that the original derives much of its effect from the rhymes Cros finds for *violon*.

Included here are all of the monologues Cros left, 21 of them, preceded by the two versions of "The Salt Herring." I've added Coquelin's performance notes, mentioned above, and two columns by Alphonse Allais: an obituary and a defense of Cros's phonograph. There are notes tucked away in the back, which offer scintillating data on the original publications and explain the occasional topical or stubbornly Gallic reference. Cros's characters travel a great deal, throughout Paris and elsewhere; I glossed only a few places that seemed particularly relevant.

As is too often the case, Cros has been received more favorably after his death then before. A posthumous collection of poetry and prose, *Le Collier de Griffes* (*The Claw Necklace*) was published in 1908 to critical acclaim. André Breton and his band of acolytes championed Cros in the heyday (hey, hey!) of Surrealism. "The Salt Herring" is now routinely recited by sullen French schoolchildren. The French equivalent of the US Recording Academy is named the Académie Charles Cros; even Brigitte Bardot recorded him ("Sidonie," with music by Giannis Spanos). English translations, however, are few and scattered. Kenneth Rexroth translated some of the poems, but the monologues, for some reason, have lain untouched. They're still performed in France; maybe some intrepid anglophone actors will take them for a spin. At any rate, here they are. I think they're wonderful, and if you don't like them, I'll never speak to you again.

Doug Skinner
New Paltz, NY
August, 2018

RHYTHMIC STORY FOR LITTLE CHILDREN

There was a great white wall, bare, bare, bare,
Against the wall, a ladder, high, high, high,
And on the ground, a salt herring, dry, dry, dry,
And a thin string, long, long, long,
With a big iron nail, sharp, sharp, sharp,
And finally a hammer, heavy, heavy, heavy.

(*A pause.*)
He comes, and takes in his hands, dirty, dirty, dirty,
Nail, herring, hammer, string—all, all, all.
Then he climbs the ladder, high, high, high,
He lifts the hammer, heavy, heavy, heavy,
And hammers in the iron nail: toc, toc, toc,
High on the great white wall, bare, bare, bare,
Ties to it the string, long, long, long,
And at the end, the salt herring, dry, dry, dry.

(*A half pause.*)
He descends the ladder, high, high, high,
Carries it off with the hammer, heavy, heavy, heavy,
And then he goes away, far, far, far.
Nobody ever saw him again, nobody, nobody, nobody.

(*A half pause.*)
(*Even slower, and lowering the voice.*)
And since then, the salt herring, dry, dry, dry,
At the end of that string, long, long, long,
Has been swinging very slowly, (*gesture*) forever, forever, forever.

(*A pause.*)
I wrote this story, simple, simple, simple,
To amuse children, little, little, little.

(*Indicate with your hand the diminishing heights of the children.*)

THE SALT HERRING

To Guy

There was a great white wall—bare, bare, bare,
Against the wall, a ladder—high, high, high,
And on the ground, a salt herring—dry, dry, dry.

He comes, holding in his hands—dirty, dirty, dirty,
A heavy hammer, a big nail—sharp, sharp, sharp,
A ball of string—big, big, big.

Then he climbs the ladder—high, high, high,
And hammers in the sharp nail—toc, toc, toc,
High on the great white wall—bare, bare, bare.

He drops the hammer—which falls, which falls, which falls,
Ties to the nail the string—long, long, long,
And, at the end, the salt herring—dry, dry, dry.

He descends the ladder—high, high, high,
Carries it off with the hammer—heavy, heavy, heavy,
And then he goes away—far, far, far.

And since then, the salt herring—dry, dry, dry,
At the end of that string—long, long, long,
Has been swinging very slowly—forever, forever, forever.

I wrote this story—simple, simple, simple,
To annoy adults—serious, serious, serious,
And to amuse children—little, little, little.

THE DUBOIS FAMILY

To my friend Coquelin Cadet, of the Comédie-Française

I follow another interminable boulevard, with buildings that all look alike, all covered by commerce with big gold letters. The sky was whitish, the pavement sticky, the air reeked of boredom. On one large balcony I read: "Dubois, shirtmaker," on the next balcony: "Dubois, tailor." Then, one after another, "Dubois, wholesale collars and ties," "Dubois, sewing machine parts," "Dubois…" again!

At the end of the boulevard, a station. Well, I'll buy a ticket for somewhere, anywhere. I enter the station, the train's about to leave. There were a lot of ugly people kissing each other; tears watered the overnight bags and lap robes.

"What, you here?"

It was one of my friends, his name as unknown to me as the seventeenth King of Babylon. Questions. Explanations.

"What? You never met old grandpa Dubois, the man we just took to the station? Ah! Let's go, I put in an appearance, that's enough. Speaking of which, you must have dinner with me."

I'm dragged to some long avenue in the suburbs to the sound of the following words:

"Ah! It's lucky I ran into you. I just made a date with Veloutine for this evening at Papa Isidore's (an exquisite restaurant), and she'll bring Acajou."

"Acajou?"

"Yes. You know, that tall redhead who amuses you so much. We'll have a much livelier dinner with four…"

Oh! On those days of dull boredom, to be lulled by the words of a friend who's totally vacuous!

Pulling out his watch:

"Four thirty, we have some time until five, let's get some absinthe, we'll chat a bit."

We enter a white cafe that smells like recent paint. There, while he prepares our two absinthes, my friend keeps talking.

"What! You never met old grandpa Dubois, the man we just took to the station? Well, I'll tell you just who old grandpa Dubois is. First of all he had a father, him too, like everyone else. This father had been the assessor of sales tax under Louis XV. He insinuated himself so well that he kept the position after that, through all the regimes. You don't think I knew him? It was in 1823 or '24, I was just a kid. He still wore powder, and always sniveled when he mentioned his daughter (the sister of the man we just took to the station), who died of a broken heart at nineteen. I still remember the day we buried the old blueblood. Say, it was a day just as dreary as today..."

And pushing a glass of absinthe before me:

"I can guarantee it's mixed well."

Still adding a thin stream of water to his own glass:

"You don't need to pour it from high up. (That's a myth.) You have to go slowly, slowly, and then all of a sudden, floof! You have the perfect mixture. So, his son..."

"Which son?" I said, just to look like I was talking.

"The son of the old tax assessor, this son was precisely the same old grandpa Dubois we just took to the station. He was married in 1814 or 1815. Was it a marriage of convenience or love? My word, I have no idea. In any case, the situation was pretty much the same on both sides. And, it's a curious thing, but the young lady he married, and who was his faithful companion until last year, was named Mademoiselle... Can you guess?"

I remained mute, as if seized with anxiety.

"She was named Mademoiselle Dubois! But she wasn't related to him on either side. The Dubois family I was telling you about is from around Dijon, and this Mademoiselle Dubois (the wife of the man we just took to the station) was from a family of small landholders in Rouergue. They were a very close couple. I know quite well that at one time there was gossip about Madame Dubois; but it was later discovered that it was a cousin of hers in Rouergue, angry that he hadn't married her, who was spreading false rumors. They had a son who died, when he left school, where he'd been a rather good student, just as he was entering law school without much idea of finishing. He planned to become an administrator. Because he died of a chill; say, I still remember the day we buried him. It was in '32 or '33, a dreary day like today. The loss always affected old grandpa Dubois. He was telling me about it only a week ago. But he still loves his daughter, Madame Dubois, the mother, whom we can go visit for a game of checkers some evening, if you like."

"What do you mean, Madame Dubois?"

"Of course! Madame Dubois, the mother, formerly Mademoiselle Dubois, the mother of all the other Dubois (the daughter of the man we just took to the station); and who married a certain Dubois, who wasn't related to her in any way, because he came from Gâtinais (his family is well known in Melun). Say, I still remember the day of the wedding; it was in fact a really dreary day like today. I had brand-new polished shoes, and they hurt!"

At that moment, my friend interrupts himself.

"Five twenty-five, let's go to dinner now. Veloutine promised to be there at five thirty." The restaurant is only ten steps away… "Waiter, a table for four in a private room!" cries my friend, turning to me.

Acajou and Veloutine have not yet arrived; we wait for them with our feet under the table, drinking Madeira.

In the next room, we hear laughter and the clatter of spoons.

As soon as we're seated, my friend continues:

"So, Madame Dubois, the mother, married a certain Dubois from Gâtinais. He's a peaceful man who married partly for affection, partly for convenience. Besides, she brought as a dowry (her grandfather was well connected) a position as tax collector in Gonesse. They had three children. First a daughter who died at twenty-one…"

"Of a broken heart, I suppose?"

"Well! Did you know her?"

"No, but I can guess."

"It's curious that you guessed that, you. The older son was a fairly good student, and entered law school. Ah! I have to tell you that this Dubois family lives in Paris, and that father Dubois turned his position over to a certain… a certain Dubois, in fact, that he didn't know from Adam. Eight years ago, the older Dubois son graduated from high school. It was a really dreary day like today. I was all muddy when I got to their house for dinner. It was a charming evening. You could already see the young graduate's interest in the young lady he later married. What was my surprise when, at my request, they told me the name of the young woman who had just been singing (and rather well, I must say), accompanied by her mother on the piano."

"Her name was Dubois," I said, my eyes glazing over.

"How did you guess? But you know them quite well. You surprise me… Five forty-five! Too bad, let's start on the soup, maybe that will bring them.

"Yes indeed, that evening was truly charming, except for one thing, the younger brother wasn't there. You know, he quarreled with his family."

"What younger son? What family???!!!"

"Are you joking?"

"Oh, no!"

"The younger Dubois son, the other grandson of the man we just took to the station, who spells his name D apostrophe Ubois, and who hangs around artists' studios… (but it's for the models)… The ladies are decidedly very late, let's go ahead and have dinner; we can watch them eat if they show up."

Although I was completely stupefied, the fumes from the absinthe, the Madeira, and the dinner made me follow with fierce attention every detail about the Dubois family.

"I sometimes visit the older Dubois and his wife. They have a little daughter of four, who's the very portrait of the grandfather, the man we just took to the station. Their little boy, on the other hand, is a little pale…"

"What little boy?" and I tore at my breast with my nails.

"The brother of the little girl. They hope to have him study law after high school, but he may not make it that far; with a constitution like his, all it takes…"

I groaned. "All it takes is a chill," I screamed, furious that I clutched in my hand only a fruit knife that couldn't cut.

At those words, we heard from the next room:

"But you've had too much Chartreuse, Veloutine."

"It's not me, it's Acajou."

My friend arose, white as a sheet, left, returned, then, falling into his chair:

"Oh! It's that Dubois with an apostrophe who stole our ladies!"

When we left the restaurant, the fresh air of the street revived me a bit. "I leave you," my friend said. "Come see me one of these days. Here's my new address." I took the card, and when he sees me look stunned, he added: "Ah, but I'm not related to them."

"Me neither, nor to you, for I too am named Dubois."

THE RUE BEAUBOURG AFFAIR

THE LAWYER, THE VICTIM: M. Coquelin Cadet

To Coquelin Cadet

THE LAWYER (*eloquently*)

And besides, gentlemen of the court, gentlemen of the jury, yes, we have murdered, even basely murdered, with premeditation, with cunning. And if the victim survived our attack, it's too bad... (*Correcting himself.*) It is the work of Providence, whose ways are inscrutable.—Now, I call on each of you, gentlemen of the court, gentlemen of the jury... Only a moment ago you saw the victim take the stand, his wounds completely healed. What did this failed victim say? Oh, my God! Nothing bad! Have creatures like him ever thought anything good, or bad? You saw him introduce himself with that beatific expression particular to the incompetent, you saw a pale reflection of those fashionable types we find so amusing in plays and songs. (*He hums a few measures of "A Man for Amanda."*) I saw—don't deny it!—bewilderment and then profound boredom on your faces when, idly, with a vacant stare, he removed his monocle... which is useless, because he's not near-sighted: Well, permit me, the better to refresh your memory on the salient points of this affair... Permit me, I say, gentlemen of the court, gentlemen of the jury, to recite for you, even imitating his voice, the words spoken by the victim in his testimony:

THE VICTIM

(*in a somewhat dithering tone*)

My God, Your Honor, it's quite simple, I have no idea why this man who was my friend, and who is still my friend...

THE LAWYER

At the hearing, you saw my client shudder at that word.

THE VICTIM

Who is still my friend, tried to make an attempt on my life. Both of us were good chums for six months. We saw each other every day. I arrived at his house at about eight in the morning, and started chatting, for I must tell you that I love to chat. (I'm like that.) I usually told him what I'd done the day before; it's true that he'd been with me almost all the time: but he's so distracted that you'd swear he doesn't see or hear a thing that happens when we're together. And besides, I also told him what I'd done after I left him: not much, because I left as late as possible, and also what I'd seen in the morning from the time I woke up to when I got to his house. You know, Your Honor, adventures like those in a novel don't happen to everyone. They never happened to me. (I'm like that.) But, on the contrary, almost every day there are bizarre coincidences in my life. So, for example, I saw, I don't know how many times, at the turning of rue Beaubourg, on my way to the accused, an odd-numbered cab drawn by a white horse. It was like the hand of fate. But by no means did it happen every day! So when I saw one, I said to my friend—I mean the accused—this morning I saw my odd-numbered cab and its white horse, it's bizarre; when I didn't see one, I said to him: this morning I didn't see either an odd-numbered cab or a white horse at the turning of rue Beaubourg, it's bizarre.

THE LAWYER

Gentlemen of the court, gentlemen of the jury, this regimen lasted for six months!

THE VICTIM

On the day of the attack, I was at his house in the morning, as usual—that is to say, no, no, that day it was a little earlier, around seven fifteen, seven twenty. He was asleep, I woke him up and found him a little unhappy; so I started chatting a bit to amuse him. That morning, as it happened, I had seen two cabs with white horses, at the turning of rue Beaubourg, but one was even-numbered, it was bizarre. I told him about that first, and then I told him what I'd done the night before. I remember that at that point my friend, (*correcting himself*) the accused got up and started stropping his razor on the leather strap... he even put paste on it.

THE LAWYER

Gentlemen, if I tell you all this, it's to show you how regrettable it is that the victim survived.

THE VICTIM

When you left so suddenly last night—he had, in fact, left quite suddenly—it was a quarter to nine, twenty to nine. I had been to 47 rue Montmartre, to see a sock maker, to tell him to deliver the half dozen I ordered at seven o'clock sharp today. I like my orders delivered promptly. (I'm like that.) The sock maker told me he was late because his employee had had to go to Ternes to deliver a gross of shorts to a former haberdasher who had retired from business, and who, I believe, wants to start again. When I left the sock maker, it was nine ten, nine fifteen, I took the bus back home—do you know that it was very humid last night? I try to light a match, it won't catch; the second one won't catch either, the third one catches, but goes out. Just think, my housekeeper had put the candlestick by the open window, finally one catches—one match, I mean. I light my candle, which sputters a bit—gets lower, lower, and then goes out. So I choose the dryest matches, and I go to the cupboard, where I always keep a box of candles. (I'm like that.) I don't know why the accused, who was my friend—and still is my friend—found anything wrong with what I said about all that. He came toward me, clutching the razor he'd just shaved with, he looked at me intently, and then put it back in the case. I paid no attention at the time; but thinking about it later, it seems he already meant me harm. (I often think about things later.) (I'm like that.) When he was dressed, we left together, to work up a little appetite before lunch; me, I like to chat while I walk. I chatted a lot that morning to amuse the accused, who bacame more and more bizarre, his eyes seemed to pop out of his head, and his face was red, red. So, from that moment on, and during lunch, he who never said anything, he started constantly interrupting me to recite a lot of tragedies, comedies, I don't even know what. It lasted all day. Finally, ten minutes before dinnertime, at ten to six, he suddenly stopped, he looked miserable, and he'd lost his voice.

Then, because he wasn't eating, I started chatting to amuse him: This morning, I woke up at six, six fifteen, it was still dark out. I put on my pants and slippers, because my housekeeper doesn't come until six thirty to make me some cafe au lait and to shine my shoes. I washed my feet in cold water. (I'm like that.) And besides, in this weather, it's not dangerous for anyone. After that, I started brushing my waist-coat, because I've noticed that my housekeeper brushes my coat well, brushes my pants well, brushes my hat well, but... He didn't let me finish. "This has gone on for six months, it's too much!" he said in a low voice. It was then that he threw himself on me, he seemed very happy, I thought he was joking; but he grabbed my nose, squeezed it vigorously, and tried to kill me by stabbing me in the ear with an oyster fork! I cried murder! He was arrested; but even if you convict him, he'll always be my friend.

(A pause.)

THE LAWYER (joyfully)

We thank the gentlemen of the court, the gentlemen of the jury, for the unanimous acquittal that has just been pronounced, but in expressing all our gratitude to the jury, we pose the secondary question of imprisonment, as a precaution, for the supposed victim (in the interest of protecting the public), and we urge that the question be decided forthwith.

(A pause.)

THE LAWYER
(throwing himself into his client's arms)

He's in prison! We're saved!

THE TRIP TO (DOT DOT DOT)

A TRAVELER: M. Coquelin Cadet

The scene takes place in ..., in the present day.

THE TRAVELER

(*He enters quickly.*)

Excuse me, gentlemen, if I'm late. It's because I just returned from traveling. What a charming little trip I took! Just picture a village, no, a town, a large town even, one hour, two hours, three hours at the most, from Paris. (I don't remember the exact distance, because I forgot to check the time when I left, and even when I arrived: and besides, I slept through the whole train ride.) First of all, I left on business... well, that wouldn't interest you. I took my little valise, because me, I always leave big suitcases on the train or somewhere; so I keep my little valise in my hand (*gesture*), and it never leaves me, I board the train, I get off the train, and as you can see, I still have it. (*Looks in astonishment back and forth from his hand to the audience.*) This is the first time that's happened. Bah! It must still be in the station, I'll go look for it in a minute. It's easy to find a valise made of leather, no, you know, some kind of cloth. There are lots of nails, yes, lots of nails around it; I'll find it; it must be in the station I just came from, they'll recognize me. It's the northern station, no! The eastern, no! The western... Well, I don't know. I didn't come from a port town, I don't know the points of the compass... In port towns, they can wet a finger, stick it in the air, and say, it's south-south-west; well, that's their business! The station I mean is at the end of a long street with a lot of cars. It's frightening how many cars there are on that street!... Well, I'll remember the name in a minute. I have to, to get my valise back. (*Looking at his empty hand.*) Believe me, this is the first time this has happened!

So I took the northern... Anyway, never mind, and off we went. It's very nice on that side. All along the route, it's probably very nice too, but I fell asleep after the first station. The first station is... Ah! I remember the name... It's something-circle. That will help us find the station.

Ah, if you like to travel, you must go there. Me, I adore traveling, especially like that. I slept!!! I heard them calling out names ending in "ville" and "val" and "gny." I have no memory for names, however you can be sure that I remembered the place I was going to. It's?... What is it? It's on the tip of my tongue. (It's such a pretty little place!) Well, I'll tell you in a minute. So, I woke up and got off the train. Ah! You should go there, it's very picturesque.

My God, the station, you know, it's a bit like every other station. It's nice all the same. There's a sort of hangar made of painted wood, all open on the side by the track; there's a bench all around, inside, and then posters in all colors; can you picture it? Red posters, blue, green, yellow... It's a very pretty effect.

There's a little bus that goes into town, which is a few minutes away.

Ah, traveling is so much fun! Especially that place. You can imagine that on the bus I admired the countryside... It's very picturesque around there. On the right, there are fields, fields... of alfalfa... of wheat... or barley, me, I don't know about plants, that's the farmer's business. Some people see plants, and tell you: that's barley, that's oats, that's clover. Me, I don't know about all that. However, there on the right, I can assure you there's a lot of alfalfa; it's a very pretty effect; it's very picturesque... And then the bus takes a road, a road like any other... not really like any other, no! There's a house, a little white house with green shutters. You have no idea how pretty green shutters are on a little white house.

On the left... Wait! I can see it now... On the left are more fields, also alfalfa. The fields on the right, the fields on the left, all that alfalfa, it's very pretty, it's very picturesque, believe me.

The bus lets you off at the hotel, the main hotel on the town square; it's the Golden Sun? No, the Golden Lion? No... Anyway, it's golden something.

I know there's another hotel next to it, something golden too; but you have to go to the one I'm talking about, it's better; you'll recognize it, go there for me. The people who run it are very nice; I didn't have to worry about a thing, right away they gave me a room on the second floor... on the third, I don't know. If you go there, ask for that room.

It's number 7, no… 3, no, I don't remember, but they'll give it to you, they're so nice. It's a very clean room.

The maid took my valise; (it's annoying that I forgot it, I have to go look for it in a minute). She's not bad… that maid. How nicely she said: "Good day, monsieur. Did you have a good trip?" And what eyes! You know, whether her eyes were blue, black, green, I have no idea. Do I pay attention to eye color? There are people who can tell you a woman is tall, short, she's blonde, she's brunette. What difference does it make? As long as she's nice! Me, I never remember all those details.

You must take that room when you get there. It's clean! First of all, there's a bed with white curtains, there are white curtains on the window too; there's a table, then there are two… No! Three chairs. Ah! There's also an armchair; the armchair, in fact, is a little hard, but when you travel you can't be too fussy about that.

The maid opened the window… (She's not bad at all, that maid.) She opened the window for a little air… There's a very pretty view; it looks out on the town square; you're right across from the Commerce Cafe, no! The Union, no! The Progress, I think. It's the most suitable cafe in the area. I went down to the cafe before dinner; there were a lot of people. You'll have to go to that cafe. You'll recognize it, there's a billiard table. That's where you'll see the customs of the place, the clothes, etc. So there were people there in blue overalls, and others with overcoats. They wear funny clothes in that region. But after all, the clothes are nice. They're very good people… I listened to them discussing their business matters. They discuss things well; they talked about, my God, you know, the price of grain and hay, buying and selling livestock, cattle, calves, at so much percent. There was a tall man in overalls, with a whip; I think he was a horse-trader, because I heard him say: "When I buy a horse, I want it to be a horse, because if it's not a horse!… Me, I want a horse."

Believe me, it's a very pretty little area. You should go there. After that, I had dinner at the hotel, at the table d'hôte. Maybe you don't know what that is, a table d'hôte? It's very curious, especially that one. Go and see it, go there for me. It's a table in a long dining room, a table shaped like a rectangle… No! I think the one I'm talking about is round, or rather oval; anyway, it doesn't matter; me, I eat just as well at a square table as a round table.

[There were very good people there, people from… You know, the main township around there?]

I don't remember what we ate! There was soup and then meat; anyway, we ate very well. We talked, but talked nicely.

[You know, about… about what, exactly? Well, I don't remember the subject of our conversation. I remember that the man across from me thought I disagreed with him; so he stopped talking, and ate with his nose in his plate.]

The conversation became pretty lively at the end; I would have stayed, but the bus to the station came to pick me up, I had to leave immediately on business. You know how it is… Anyway, that wouldn't interest you. I had eaten too fast. I was sleepy! And believe me, I made myself comfortable as soon as I was seated in the train. And coming back, just imagine: I fell asleep again in the car that brought me here.

(*He pulls out his watch.*)

But now, it's half past. Oh, I don't know the hour. My watch keeps perfect time, but only has one hand, the big one, for the minutes. It doesn't matter, there's still time for me to go look for my valise. But how can I find the station?… Ah! I'll ask a coachman… And with a good tip… (*He feels in his pockets.*) But where's my wallet?… It must be in my valise! Well, if you hear anything about that valise, it's leather… cloth, with nails, lots of nails, write me at number… on rue… Oh, damn! Well, it doesn't matter, write me; I'm well known in the neighborhood. (*He leaves, and returns to say:*) Be sure to put my first name on it, because the man upstairs has the same last name as me.

(NOTE: The lines in brackets were cut in performance.)

THE BILBOQUET

To Coquelin Cadet

But no! It would bore you. It's the kind of thing that happens to all artists. All right! I'll tell you about it in a few words (*He takes out his watch and checks the time.*) because I have to get to work.

It was on a Sunday, near the Bastille, in the business district; there are wide sidewalks and trees full of dust. The shops were just closing. Concierges were sitting before their buildings, to inhale the aroma of the cab stand. And they call that getting fresh air! And then a lot of people returning from the country; they were exhausted, they carried big bouquets of wildflowers, and baskets clattering with tin cans, bread crusts, and empty bottles. There were also girls playing badminton before their parents' shops, you know, kerosene lamp dealers, little grocers, druggists… Well, it was there that I noticed a ring of people, gaping like steamed clams around a little druggist: a boy of fifteen or sixteen, with a mop of dirty blond hair, staring eyes, swollen cheeks, and big hands. This brat stood there like an idiot playing… Guess what? Bilboquet! Ah! He'd caught the ball nineteen times! And he kept going, counting, "twenty, twenty-five, thirty…" He attracted a crowd… even the girls playing badminton stopped to come see him! He was a success.

Carried away by fame, the little man goes on to other tricks; he catches the ball and balances it on the spike. He holds the ball in his hand. Now it's the bilboquet that goes flying and plants itself on the ball. Murmurs of approval from the audience! Then the young artist catches the bilboquet in the air, and spikes the ball on it, then catches the ball and nabs the bilboquet, and continues in that vein awhile, and to end with something remarkable—he knows his audience—he takes out his knife, cuts the cord, and by concentrated movements of his wrist, frees the ball, which spins, and invariably lands on the spike…

It was then that I stopped him: I'd had enough!! I said to him, "Do you think you're playing bilboquet, my young friend?" I took his bilboquet from him. "What do you have here?… It doesn't have the right weight for a beginner, it doesn't have the precision for a correct game, you'll just lose your touch with this tree branch!" I tried the ball, letting it roll down my arm; the center of gravity wasn't aligned with the hole! He stared at me with huge eyes, he had no idea what a center of gravity was, and he wanted to be a bilboquetist!

I told him: "Throw this in the fire! You have to develop your arm for at least six months, with a Thompson bilboquet, in aluminum bronze." (*To the audience.*) The platinum ones are excellent, but too expensive for a druggist. "Yes, six months, at least, of practice with the Thompson. That's what I did, gentlemen, and not for six months, but three years; after those three years I knew nothing; I had strength, I had a powerful arm, but... I knew nothing, less than nothing.

"So I went on to the Schutzenberger bilboquet, in ebony, with an ivory ball—the ball isn't made by Schutzenberger, but by Cascarini, in Bologna. Cascarini makes the best balls in the world, but doesn't understand handles, besides, he stopped making them. But for bilboquet handles, there's nobody like Schutzenberger, I mean the ones before 1817, the signed ones! Because the new ones are hacked out with a billhook. I know full well there's Van der Dussen the elder, in Rotterdam, who imitates Schutzenberger, not badly even, but you can only find them used, and because they're inexpensive, they've been played badly, and when a bilboquet has been played badly! Pfsst! (*Gesture.*) As for those Belgian imitations by Jean Moërickx, they're poorly adjusted, poorly centered, they won't do! Ah! Then too, in Ravennes there was a maker, an artist named Giambattista Farone, he's excellent at setting and retouching.

"As for the cord, that's a whole other matter! The only decent cord in the world is made by Juan Fonseca in Lisbon. He steeps it... soaks it... marinates it, for two hours, no longer, in green vitriol, then dries it and lubricates it with walnut oil kept in a very dry place.

"And then there's the way you stretch it over the copper spindle, and wind it onto the oval reel. Anyway, I have the formulas and tools at home—you won't find them anywhere else.

"And then fitting the cord onto the handle of the bilboquet! And fitting it to the ball! You don't know how, you'll never know! I don't know, myself. It doesn't matter, come see me, and I'll attach it for you."

Many people there seemed to take no interest in what I was saying; but there are some things no artist can ignore! So I told the boy what I'd done: "I worked for six months, three years, with a Thompson, but what I call working! I got up every morning at six. A half hour for my toilette. A half hour to eat my soup and take a little exercise. Always soup! Never cafe au lait or other stimulants that ruin the stability of the nerves. At seven o'clock, seven fifteen, I was at work. Ah! When ten o'clock rolled around, my arm was often sore (*Gesture.*), but I continued until ten thirty. Then I stopped working, and used the half hour until eleven for an icy shower, and a rub-down with coarse gray salt to prevent stiffness. From eleven thirty to noon, I took a fairly long walk. At noon, I had lunch. Every day, soup and beef with a plate of vegetables. Sometimes a little sweet for dessert. Very little wine, never any coffee! After lunch, I took another little walk; me, I like my comforts.

"But at one o'clock, I was back at work until four. At four o'clock, another cold shower (without a rub-down) and a bite of dry bread. And there I am again with my instrument until seven. And then dinner—oh, just a light meal; and a little walk. I've noticed that a certain amount of leisure in the evening opens the mind to new combinations. Practice isn't everything in art, you need to dream! At ten thirty or later, to bed. I kept the bilboquet beside me, on my nightstand, in case of sudden ideas or insomnia. I did that every day that God made, for ten years, and after ten years, I knew nothing! Truly nothing! Rigorously nothing! I didn't give up, I got back to work for another ten years. (We can learn nothing, we know nothing)...

"I who speak to you now, I know nothing! You'll tell me I won first prize in the great international contest in 1858. You know, with the Americans? But with no serious competitors! I won't be the one to mention that contest!"

I said to that young man: "Quit your drugstore at once. Do as I did for ten years, twenty years, you'll know nothing. Don't give up, persevere, and you'll know nothing! Nothing! Nothing! Besides, what can you hope for if you spend every day selling linseed meal and enemas?... It's unworthy of your aspirations! If your parents (his mother, a big fat woman, glared angrily at me), if your parents can do without you and assure you of six or seven hundred francs a year (I don't have much more than that, myself), do nothing but work with your bilboquet, not that one, not that bowling pin. If you don't have the vocation, you'll never get anywhere. And if you do have it, you won't get any further, but you'll work to be like me, to know that you know nothing!"

Just imagine, that young idiot holds out his bilboquet to see me play with it. "Ah!" I replied. "Do you think I'd use a chair leg like that? And on the sidewalk, too, in front of people whom I... respect as one should respect all people, but who have neither concentration nor taste. Taste! Which is necessary for any serious presentation. Play bilboquet on the sidewalk? Exhibit myself like a street singer? That would be to lose all artistic dignity." (*To the audience.*) I don't even want to play it here, because I'd be ashamed of your approval, given my absolute worthlessness! For I'm worthless! I know nothing! I'm worthless! Worthless! Worthless! Worthless! I know nothing! Nothing!! Nothing!!!

(*He exits with his arms upraised, exasperated.*)

THE MAID

Sketch

THE MAID: Mlle. Jeanne Samary.
Accessories: a feather duster, an apron.

A living room.

How hard it is anyway to keep a good position!

I've only been here a week. It's the first time I've worked as a servant. It was the postmistress back home who recommended me to Madame.

Ah! How stupid I must have looked when I got here!

Madame doesn't seem very friendly: and yet she's a good person, Madame is; except when she's in a bad mood, like last night.

I got here, it was three o'clock, Madame showed me the work to be done; her room, dust the Tunisian curios on the top shelf; not Mademoiselle's room, Mademoiselle has to do that herself, so she'll learn good habits for when she gets married. And that's it.

The rest concerns the cook, who has such pockmarks! But a nice girl. Just imagine, she makes my beds, she sweeps for me. She doesn't want me to wear myself out, so my only work is dusting the Tunisian curios, even if I broke a little statue yesterday. No harm done, it was so ugly.

Ah, yes! She's a nice girl, that cook. She buys me perfume at the shop. In the morning, she brings me my coffee, and then she does my hair, she's like my own chambermaid. When I get rich, I'll hire her... as a cook! Because it would be sad to have a chambermaid with such pockmarks!

So, Madame told me to go fix myself up to answer the door if anyone calls. The bell rang, Madame told me: "It's Monsieur coming home. He comes back every day at five." I went to open the door. He looked so serious, Monsieur!

He hasn't been decorated, but he looks just like a man who's been decorated. I helped him take off his overcoat; but I was so scared! He looked so serious, and besides he's of a certain age, because M. Eugène, his older son, the one who's in business, is twenty-six, Mademoiselle is nineteen, and M. Jules, who's about to leave on vacation, will be seventeen.

There were a lot of people at dinner; two gentlemen, M. Dubois, Monsieur's friend, his friend from childhood, and then M. Oscar; I think they want him to marry Mademoiselle.

After dinner, M. Eugène, Monsieur's older son, the one who's in business (he has big black sidewhiskers; he looks almost as serious as Monsieur; he's twenty-six!), M. Eugène left. He asked me for the candle to light his big cigar. He looked at me with his eyes all funny. He came toward me. I dropped the candlestick, the candle-ring broke, I pushed the door open, M. Jules (the one about to leave on vacation) came in... I told him the wind broke the candle-ring; but he told his mother it was his fault. He's so nice, M. Jules. It's too bad they're sending him off tomorrow to his aunt in Les Andelys.

I ask you, what can a tall handsome boy of seventeen (he has such pretty eyes!) do in Les Andelys with his aunt? He'd have a much better time in Paris on his vacation, and he's so bored at the brainery (that's what he calls his school, the brainery). There's someone who's not proud, at least; he's even I don't know how to put it; he won't look at you when he talks to you; I think he grew up too fast. It's too bad, he has such pretty eyes.

In the evening, Madame took up her embroidery and Mademoiselle her crochet. Monsieur, M. Dubois (his friend from childhood), and M. Oscar (the one they want to marry Mademoiselle) started playing cards, but they talked about a dummy, I thought it was one of the tenants in the building, but it's part of the game, it's called the dummy; what do I know!

M. Jules (the one who's going on vacation) came to the kitchen to smoke cigarettes. Oh! He made us laugh with his stories! We were having dinner with the cook (it's too bad about her pockmarks). He told us he went riding every Thursday. Next year he's coming to Paris to be a student. Madame rang for me, and M. Jules left, since she doesn't want him smoking in the kitchen.

I brought the tea. Monsieur was talking very loudly with M. Dubois (his friend from childhood). Madame said M. Dubois was right, and M. Oscar (the one who's going to marry Mademoiselle) said M. Dubois was wrong. Mademoiselle didn't say anything, because she was counting her crochet stitches.

Monsieur and M. Dubois argue like that every night, but they can't do without each other.

Often, before dinner, Madame is in a bad mood because M. Dubois is late, and Monsieur asks: "Dubois isn't here yet?" But M. Dubois never fails to arrive just as we're sitting down at the table. After tea, this M. Dubois (Monsieur's friend from childhood) left with M. Oscar (the one who's going to marry Mademoiselle). I lit their way. At the door, they looked at me. They said something to each other, I don't know what, and started laughing; but I kept my distance, since I was afraid I'd break another candle-ring. M. Dubois came toward me; and then suddenly... he got such a stupid look on his face... so stupid!... Madame was behind me, and called me. Both of them ran off, and quicker than that!

Madame told me I shouldn't joke with the gentlemen, that M. Dubois had bad manners and I shouldn't listen to him.

Ah! I have to say she has nothing to worry about, Madame, with her M. Dubois! After all, he has rheumatism and a wig!

Oh! No, me I'm just a maid, but I wouldn't want a mug like that, even though he's a gentleman.

Can you believe it, he offered me a lot of money and sugared almonds. He must think I'm a monkey!

Oh! The next night I got quite a fright! My room is at the end of the hall; it's very clean, my little room; I set it up very nicely, I made a garden there with a tiny little China rose and a pot of basil. The cook cleans it for me every day (it's too bad about her pockmarks).

There's a ladder in the hall next to the wooden chest, you know a little stepladder for changing the curtains on the windows.

It was half past midnight when bang bang boom! I hear the ladder fall on the wooden chest. I give a loud scream; and I hear Monsieur's voice, saying: "What an idea, leaving that ladder in the hall!"

Madame came; she asked Monsieur what he was doing in the hall without a light. That's true, what was he doing in the hall?

They went away, Madame looked angry, and she talked loudly like when she's in a bad mood.

After that, Madame came back with a candle and knocked on my door, I let her in, she seemed to be searching my room, she looked me in the eye and left, saying I should be asleep at that hour; as if it's easy to sleep with ladders falling on wooden chests all night... What a funny house!... But I don't know how I can chatter away like this after what happened yesterday and today. Oh! I don't know what will become of me! I'm so afraid!...

First of all, yesterday morning, Monsieur shaved himself (it's true that he does it every day, and cuts himself... You know, such a serious man). And then, before breakfast, he met me in the hall... Oh! He asked me if I wanted a kiss from a clean shaven man! I was scared! I ran away!... Imagine, such a serious man! (*She jumps.*) There you go, I just heard him blowing his nose.

At breakfast, they decided that Madame would go to Gonesse. She said it was for Mademoiselle's marriage. Mademoiselle is with her aunt in Les Andelys. After coffee, M. Dubois (Monsieur's friend from child-hood) came up, just like that, to ask if I was going with Madame. I told him yes, just to see; he seemed very pleased, and put his hand in his pocket; I bet he wanted to give me more money or sugared almonds. So I told him it wasn't true, and that I was staying, and ran off.

Oh, no! I don't like that man; with his wig, he looks like he's stuffed... and besides, he puts funny smells on himself. M. Oscar (Mademoiselle's intended) wants me to go to Les Andelys; but I won't; because I have my work to do here. (You know, the Tunisian curios on the shelf.) (*She jumps.*) Monsieur blew his nose again!

I'd be glad to go to Les Andelys, not for M. Oscar, but because of M. Jules, who's finishing his vacation, and must be so bored.

He's so stupid, M. Oscar, he told me that when he and Mademoiselle get married, he'll hire me as a chambermaid for Mademoiselle; that is, for Madame Oscar. But I don't want to. M. Oscar is too stingy. He always asks me how much this or that cost, how much I'm paid; how much it costs to rent the apartment.

Should he be worrying about all that when he's in love with Mademoiselle?

Yes! Everyone wanted to take me to the country, even Madame; but Monsieur didn't like the idea; he said there'd be no one here to do the work.

He doesn't know the cook does most of it. (What a nice girl, but those pockmarks!) It doesn't matter, I'm afraid to stay here all alone with the cook and Monsieur (such a serious man!).

Especially tonight. I'm still thinking about that ladder falling on the wooden chest. (*She jumps.*) He blows his nose too much. What's wrong with a serious man like him, that he has to blow his nose all the time? Oh! I'll go find the cook, I'll be less afraid.

Even M. Eugène, Monsieur's oldest son, left on a business trip!

Besides he's not the one to make me less scared here, since he's almost as serious as his father (at twenty-six!)

Fortunately the cook hasn't gone to bed yet. She often comes in the evening to ask if I need anything.

Last night, they had an argument; M. Dubois had his rheumatism, and said he wouldn't go to Gonesse. (He looked at me when he said that! What do I care?) Monsieur told him he needed to get some rest at home, and to keep warm. Madame was in a bad mood. She left this morning telling me she'd be back this evening on the eleven o'clock train; but I'm afraid she won't come back, because I heard she has to stay for five days; I'd much rather she came home.

Ah! I'm so afraid! Monsieur had such a look on his face this morning when he shaved, I don't understand anything, you know, about such a serious man.

Oh! But now I remember; the cook is off today. She'll be away too! Oh! I'm scared! There you go! Monsieur is blowing his nose again! Oh, no! I want to leave. But where can I go?

And the concierge?... I hear his footsteps! It's Monsieur... Such a serious... And he's coming here! My room doesn't have a lock. Ladders will start falling again. Oh la la! The window's too high. Oh, too bad! Such a serious...

(*Listening.*) There's the doorbell. It's Madame's voice... she's in a bad mood... and M. Dubois. (*Jumping.*) Oh! Now I don't care, they can all blow their noses!

THE CAPITALIST

THE CAPITALIST: M. Coquelin Cadet
To Coquelin Cadet

(*Like a man in a hurry.*)

I'm very bothered. I come here to ask your advice; and do answer me quickly, because I've invested the greater part of my capital, it's true, but I still have a sum of two million five hundred thousand francs, without counting the interest that accrues, that accrues, that accrues while I talk to you, and which is not paid, at the rate of six percent (you invest at seven, even eight in business); but I'm not demanding, I'd be happy with five, but only in sure investments. Those are the only ones I make.—I'd rather lose on a sure investment than profit from a risky one.

You think it's fun to be a capitalist. It's true, sometimes it's fun, but you never have a moment to yourself!! All your capital has to be engaged.—And it's difficult! People don't want capital; no one wants money; so your money sleeps and then you can't sleep!—A roast turkey can wait; a bride (no comparison) can wait at the altar; a mother (no comparison either) can wait for her son who won't come back from the war, she can wait; only money can't wait!

And I have those two million five hundred thousand francs that have earned nothing since I've been talking to you. Quick, give me advice, but serious advice.

Someone suggested government bonds. Put money on the government! You can say, on a table; you can say, on the floor, and you know what it means;—but on the government, what's that? It's an abstraction, there's no one named the government.—It's metaphysics, the government.—It's not practical. A revolution, and what's left?

Trade, boats, ships!—That's all on the sea,—on the water; it dances on the water! The sea, what's the sea? It's water that keeps moving, never the same water! And besides, there are boats that go on the water—that's never the same! They go away: they're big at first when you see them up close, those boats. You say to yourself: it's a good boat, it's a sound investment! And then they go away; a little dot lost on the horizon. What's left? It's not serious.

The railroad? My God, you see something like a sandy path with some rails, with usually four rails. It's solid, those rails, it's iron, it's real; but there's not much iron;—and besides there are stations too, but made of wood, of cast iron, it's just rubbish. Now you'll tell me the trains, the cars, the locomotives, the equipment... Of course, it's all very nice to see, up close. I don't deny it has value; there's more iron; radiators to warm the feet, it's solid, (and there are still none in third class, no radiators).

You say to yourself: your money is well invested there. But then the train leaves on those damn iron rails. A black dot on the horizon again. What's left? Smoke? It's not serious, it's no investment.

Buy houses, lands, fields? Because it stays in one place? But the owners of those buildings, why do they sell them? If they're good, why don't they keep them? So, they're bad, it's not serious!

Telegraphs? Wires in the country, or underwater cables.—Wires? It's exposed to filth from birds; it rusts, it eats the iron.—And besides what goes through the wires? Electricity? Is that sold by the kilo? No, it's like the government; more metaphysics!—And cables?—It gets encrusted with a lot of oysters and mussels down there. It seems like nothing, all that, and then it eats away the cable. And fish? Sharks, whales, sperm whales? If they eat the cable, do you go look for it in their stomachs? Or sue them for damages and interest? It's no investment, it's not serious!

I was advised to start a stable for racehorses. Well then! You have a horse, he's listed at twenty to one, you say to yourself: "He could break a foot." You bet against him. He's obliged to run. He wins the race, and you lose your money.—That's gambling. That's betting. Maybe with a suitable bonus for the jockeys, you could do some positive business. And if the jockeys won't take it? You're ruined. I know all about it, it's happened to me. You think everything's settled: all the horses start off; the jockeys, the reds, the greens, the blues, straddling their stirrups pass like lightning. There are posts there, they tell you who finished first, second. I'd like to believe it, but after all, mistakes can be made, one horse looks so much like another horse! Who won? They return to the stable and what's left? Bad investment.

Rivers? Canals? Tugboats? Locks? All that, it's water, it flows under bridges, it never returns.

Someone told me about a business, my God! none too important, the mud in Paris! You know, what they call sludge, that you pick up like that. (*Sweeping.*) First of all, there is none, there's no mud in Paris. There's no profit in it, because it evaporates in the dump carts… and besides the sweepers aren't watched, they put half of it in their pockets.

Mining? Big holes in the ground; where everything is dark, you can't understand anything!—The workers go down there, they wander off in all directions, 300, 600 meters underground, go try to find them; they eat up three fourths of the silver with women; they come back up and blame it on the methane! What's left? It's not serious, it's no investment.

No, deep down, when I ask your advice, it's just rhetorical—because I found an excellent affair; but positive! (*Solemn.*) It's the exploitation of the rocky masses that sit, that are scattered, on the left bank of the Yenisei. What's the Yenisei?—The Yenisei. Eh! My God, it's a river, even a big river, yes. But not a river like the others (you know with water that's always flowing?), no, no. It's like this. (*A horizontal line with the hand.*) It won't flow, it won't move, it's frozen all year! And I mean frozen!!! I'm sure of it, I went to see it myself, I spent 25,000 francs on the trip: I don't mind spending money when it's about an investment.

I went to see this amazing river that never loses a drop of water,—I touched those rocky masses (I even froze two fingers and my nose). Just picture huge stones, you bang on them, you can feel it's solid. It's enormous, enormous! You'd like to take them away, it's impossible—because of the immense mass, and besides, there's no one around. There's no one, absolutely no one. The whole area is completely white without a single house. There are bears, but they're starving;—who could they eat? There's absolutely no one! And just think that those rocky masses will stay there eternally! In a hundred years, in two hundred years! It will be the same, it will be the same rocky masses! On the same left bank of the Yenisei! The same river with the same ice that won't have moved in all that time! It's wonderful!

Now, a capital that doesn't move for a hundred years, for two hundred years, even at an extremely modest rate of interest, grows and yields unlimited profits.—I just put fifty million into that business—and while I've been talking to you, I can see clearly that the two million five hundred thousands francs I have left can't be invested any better than there!—You listened to me, you said nothing, you wasted my time, (time is money) you cost me maybe five hundred thousand francs in interest that hasn't accrued, interest, it has to move. I'm the one who has to move now, to invest my two million five hundred thousand francs in rocky masses. It's more serious than you.—You don't understand that? I have only one regret, that I came here, I'm going broke here and I'm leaving. The interest accrues... I hear it accrue, I'm going broke here, I'm leaving, I won't even say goodbye! (*He exits, upset.*)

THE FENCING MASTER

A FENCING MASTER: M. Coquelin Cadet

I am a fencing master. At the moment I have no students. I don't know what's wrong with people today, they don't fight anymore, you have to fight each other. If you don't fight a little, what happens to society? No more civilization, no more progress, nothing! Fight nicely, for no real reason,—but you have to fight, and you have to kill each other. Not always,—but often.

Back when I studied under my master, Lieutenant Tafta-Gomez (he was a Spaniard, you know, a sombrero) people fought over nothing,—not me, never, I was studying fencing, and not Tafta-Gomez either, he was a teacher; I mean people in society. A fly buzzed; someone tried to catch it, someone else stopped him (not on purpose), a duel! And often a man died,—and fairly often two men died. That's what I call knowing how to live.

One time, for example, there was a serious affair. Oh! That was one that couldn't be settled. It concerned the colonel's sister. I have to tell you, I was already a teaching assistant in the 297th infantry in Commercy, the home of madeleines. It was in the 297th that I was a provost for four years and six months. So, it concerned the colonel's sister; the lieutenant-colonel said the woman was this, was that; but very bad things. Someone told the colonel, who gave a good pair of slaps… to his sister; and they didn't fight… not him and the lieutenant-colonel. But if it had been over nothing, then they would have fought.—Another time there was no soup left in the pot at mess; the man they passed the pot to threatened six of his colleagues… anyway, it would take too long to tell you about it.

But come take lessons with me, people will fight again; I can feel it, it's in the air, that time will return. First of all, I've had some excellent students, from the best society. I was the one who gave lessons to the Marquis des Plates-Bandes (he lived as a foreigner in Folkestone for many years), I gave him lessons for three months. He paid me, I remember (it was in his country's money), twenty-two francs and

seventy-seven centimes as my fee;—there were days when it was sev-
enty-eight centimes because of the exchange rate. I taught him the
principles, he did very well, very well.—After three months I told him:
"Now that you're strong, Marquis, we'll have an assault!" Because I
want the principles understood before you try an assault. The marquis
knew them thoroughly—very well, very well. You can imagine how
happy he was for an assault. Because the principles always bore the customer; but they're necessary. Obviously, you have to bore the customer
enormously. He takes his stance—oh, he was good, perfectly poised.
I take my stance, he attacks me,—I parry, and give him one of those
thrusts to the collar bone. It hurts. He gets up, he rubs himself,—he
looked angry. He takes his stance again, I take mine. He wants to give
me a one, two,—I counter,—he misses the counter,—I parry, and give
him, in return, a bruise, right in the middle of the sternum,—which
is an extremely painful cut. I did that because he didn't efface himself
enough. He gets up, he rubs himself, oh, he rubbed himself a long
time! He looked at me with a funny expression. I was irritated; I told
him: "It's because you didn't efface enough, Marquis."—Without taking his stance or answering me, he tried to beat me with his foil like it
was a cane;—he completely forgot the principles. So I began to prick
him, and he tried to hit me on the head. He retreated, and I kept prick-
ing him where it hurt the most to teach him to efface properly. When
he retreated, he reached a bell pull. He rang. A domestic came in, got
between us, jumped on me, and threw me out,—and out by the sheds
and stables, in the courtyard, they counted out for me thirty-one times
twenty-two francs and seventy-six centimes, because of the exchange
rate. I haven't seen the marquis since.

Ah! I've had some excellent students,—excellent students. I remember—oh! That one, absolutely from the highest society,—he was
a Dutch baron, from Amsterdam, Baron Van-Dennefles, (he gave me,
more than twenty times, whole Dutch cheeses—you know, the round
ones, those round cheeses).—Now there's a man who learned the principles quickly, you'd think he knew them from birth. Once again, after
seven weeks, on to the assault! "En garde, Baron," I told him. He took
his stance proudly. Go to it, attack me. Dish it out like custard! I parry.
Very good. Get up. Dish it out like custard again! That time I don't

parry, and he gets me right in the heart (the red leather heart on the plastron). He was delighted! And he started attacking me. Me, I didn't want to touch him. I remembered the marquis.—Oh! He made some fine thrusts! He gave me some bold cutovers! And I could have easily split his belly open just by extending my arm. After that session he was so pleased, he gave me many more ducats, because he was paying me in Dutch money. Those foreigners have such strange habits! We continued for a week, with those assaults; but it cost him a lot. Two plastrons a session that he destroyed; he sliced them into ribbons. Then one evening—among his friends—I don't know what happened, it was over a woman... no, over cards... no, no... over a woman... unless... well, it doesn't matter. He pours a cup of boiling punch over one of his closest friends. They send seconds, they set a time for the next day, they invite me (not as a second, you know, not with a baron!)—just to carry the swords and pistols. I had three boxes of pistols and a pair of sabers, four foils, and four pairs of dueling swords. The seconds confer to reach an agreement and to arrange the affair... to have them exchange one bullet from their pistols; if that doesn't work, they'll continue with sabers; and if the opponents get too tired, they'll switch to dueling swords,—you know, those swords you can use with one hand, a toy! It's a pleasure to hold those swords. The pistols don't work; no one ends up on the ground. They skipped the sabers, and went straight to the swords; and there's my idiot of a baron starting to go pif paf on the other man's blade, he makes some cutovers, you know, like he did with me in our assault; the other one gets scared, sticks out his arm, and without meaning to, drives three inches of steel into his lower back, because the baron effaced too much.

He spent two months in bed. I went to see him every day. When he was back on his feet, he left for Amsterdam, and I never saw him again. He still owes me twenty-six ducats. If you want to buy my debt, I can let you have it for three francs and fifty centimes.

Ah! I've had some excellent students; but you don't get the best students in society anymore;—in fact, I had one who was perfect, very strong, much stronger than myself, I can assure you. He was the son of a tanner, and had joined the regiment on a whim: he enlisted. He had sold a hundred fifty kidskins that belonged to his father, to buy a watch and chain for some low woman, and then he stole the watch and chain from her. There were even some rumors about a murder; but he was my best student. So he enlisted, he joined the regiment. In the arms room, he could get the best of me whenever he wanted, all the time. Well, that boy fought with a little hunchback who knew nothing at all, who'd never even touched a foil. My student tries to give him a one two close on the outside, it was a feint, and then bring the blade back, with his fingernails up, to prick him right in the chest. The other one, the hunchback, who couldn't even hold a blade, didn't notice any of that, and gave him some opposition... was it a second match, the hand high? I don't know,—those aren't thrusts, done like that. In the end, he stabbed him, and killed my best student. It's not the man I miss (he was a scoundrel), but the beauty of his work.

Really, come take some lessons with me, my prices are quite reasonable. There's not a fencing master in Paris like me for the principles.—Take lessons with me, because they'll start fighting again in society, they'll start fighting over nothing again, it's in the air, everyone will fight now,—all of you here. That's progress; what do you expect! Progress marches on. Anyway, I have to go, I have to attend to a matter that's dragging on, I have to go there to make them fight. You have my address. You'll all fight each other, you may get killed, but above all, the principles, the principles! (*He exits, then returns.*) Ah! Excuse me. The foils, gloves, sandals, and plastrons are extra.

IN THE PAST

THE SPEAKER: M. Coquelin Cadet

Long ago—but long ago isn't strong enough to give you the idea...
But how else can I put it?

Long, long, long ago; but really long, long ago.

So, one day... No, there was no day, and no night, so once upon a
time, but there was no... Yes, once upon a time, how else can you say
it? So, he got it into his head (no, there was no head), he got the idea...
Yes, that's good, he got the idea to do something.

He wanted to drink. But drink what? There was no vermouth, no
Madeira, no white wine, no red wine, no Dreher beer, no cider, no water! What you don't realize is that it all had to be invented, that it wasn't
already made, that progress has marched on. Oh! Progress!

Since he couldn't drink, he wanted to eat. But eat what? There was
no sorrel soup, no turbot with caper sauce, no roast, no potatoes, no
pot roast, no pears, no Roquefort cheese, no indigestion, no places to
be alone... We live in progress! We think it always existed, all of that!

So since he couldn't drink or eat, he wanted to sing, (*Gaily.*), to
sing. To sing, (*Sadly.*) yes, but sing what? No songs, no romances, "My
heart! We must part!" No heart, no parting, no "Tra la la, you'll wear
yourself out!" No melody for the voice to carry, no violin, no accordion,
no organ, (*Gesture.*), no piano! You know, for the concierge's daughter
to play accompaniment on, no concierge! Oh! Progress!

Can't sing; impossible? Well then, I'll dance. But dance where? On
what? No waxed parquet, you know, to slip and fall. No evenings with
chandeliers, candelabras on the wall that drip wax on your back, wine-
glasses, cordials that you spill on dresses! No dresses! No dancers to
wear the dresses! No snoring fathers, no blotchy mothers to spoil the
fun!

So, no drinking, no eating, no singing, no dancing. What to do?—
Sleep! Well then, I'll go to sleep. Sleep, but there was no night, none of
those moments when time stands still (you know, when you yawn (*He
yawns.*), when you yawn, when you yawn in the evening).

There was no evening, no bed, no comforter, no quilt, no bowl of hot water, no nightstand, no... but enough! Oh! Progress!

So he wanted love! He said to himself: I'll fall in love; I'll sigh; it's a distraction; I'll even be jealous; I'll beat my... My what? Beat what? Who? Be jealous of what? Of whom? In love with whom? Sigh for whom? For a brunette? There were no brunettes. For a blonde? There were no blondes, or redheads; not even any hair or wigs, since there were no women!

Women hadn't been invented! Oh! Progress!

So die, then! Yes, he said to himself (*Resigned.*) I want to die. Die how? No Saint-Martin canal, no ropes, no revolvers, no illnesses, no potions, no pharmacists, no doctors!

So he wanted nothing! (*Plaintive.*) An even sadder situation!... (*Changing his mind.*) But no, don't cry! There was no situation, no unhappiness. Happiness, unhappiness, all that is modern!

The end of the story? But there was no end. Ends hadn't been invented. Ending is an invention, it's progress! Oh! Progress! Progress! (*He exits, stupefied.*)

THE REASONABLE MAN

THE REASONABLE MAN: M. Coquelin Cadet

(*He enters with a letter in his hand.*) What's this? A letter from my wife. Why did she write me? I saw her this morning. Another female idea; they exaggerate everything; I don't like exaggeration. (*He puts the letter in his pocket.*)

That's not what this is about; I came here to tell you an adventure, no, a story, no, it's not even a story, since stories never happen to me! Something that happened to me just today.—This morning, I got up feeling happy, not really happy, but anyway I felt all right. I'm not one of those people who laugh ha! ha! ha! without knowing why, or cry boo! hoo! hoo! without knowing why either. No, I'm serious,—not serious—but reasonable, yes, that's it… reasonable. It's not that I'm old. I'm even younger than I seem, without being young! You know, youth, it thinks it can do everything, it thinks everything is beautiful: "Oh, spring! Oh, flowers!" Pgt!* No, let's not exaggerate. Spring… is the end of winter, or the beginning of summer, anyway… it's spring. Nor am I like those old people who don't like this, who won't like that, who say: (*Indifferent tone.*) "Spring! Flowers!"—Well then! Flowers are on plants, they grow after the leaves, or before, on apple trees! Pgt! Let's not exaggerate. They have their place, flowers: for landscaping, for herbal tea!…!—No, I'm interrupting myself, I must tell you that I'd bought a hat with an electric lining.—It's not that I believe in inventions, but at any rate, I found the hat, the price was… reasonable. Besides, it was very… no, it was reas… no, it was suitable! So, this morning, I leave the house very… no, in good spirits, the weather was superb… no, it was all right. I say to myself: I'll buy a paper. It's not that I'm passionate about politics, because you have people who tell you: "In politics, there's only this, it must be that, it must be the other thing!…" Well, no! It's not that I'm like the others, you know, the people in the opposite party? who tell you: "It can't be this; it can't be that…" Pgt!… Let's not exaggerate! In politics, you see, you have to know… Pgt! Anyway… you shouldn't think everything is good or bad, just because someone said this or that… Anyway, you know what I mean.

So I buy my paper, I unfold it, it was very windy… no, it was windy. I fold my paper up again, because, you know, if I read it or don't read it, it's the same thing. Journalists sometimes say things are black, and sometimes white. Why would everything be white? I don't believe it. Why would everything be black? Don't believe that either.—So it was windy and the wind blew my hat: I pulled it down over my ears (my hat). I know it doesn't look good, without looking bad; because we have other ideas about what looks good and what looks bad; when your hat's down over your ears like that, you don't look handsome, you're no Apollo: it's practical; now, when something is practical, it's not ugly, I know very well that in sculpture… Oh! But if you listen to artists!… Well, I once knew a musician: all music that wasn't like his he wanted nothing to do with, he said it was bad! But let's not talk about music, we'll be here all night discussing it.

So I was walking, and my paper wasn't completely refolded. You know, because it was windy… not very windy, but windy enough. I was at the entrance to the bridge (I don't remember which bridge). I notice a little lady, to say that she was pretty… Pgt! No, let's not exaggerate, anyway, she held her dress like this (*Gesture.*), she was… (*Wink.*) No! She wasn't (*Wink.*)… anyway, you know what I mean. I'm not like those men who say to you: women, women! It's all they talk about! Nor am I like those who twirl their mustache, and say: women, women! I simply say: women.— I thought she was very nice, that little lady. I can't say I was in love with her, because there are people who say: Oh! Love, love! And then say to women: I love you! I love you! Pgt. Let's not exaggerate.

So, I held my paper in one hand, and with the other I pulled my hat down more and more over my ears, because of the wind.

I walked up like that to the little lady, you'll tell me it wasn't right for a married man! Yes! I'm married, but not really married. Oh! Legitimately, of course. No, I love my wife. Pgt! Let's not exaggerate. I esteem… no, I'm fond of my wife. And besides, I'm not one of those people who say: Marriage! Marriage! It's a sacrament! Pgt! Nor should you say: (*Indifferent.*) Marriage, marriage!

It's like being jealous, it's an exaggeration. For example, my wife has a cousin, his name is Oscar. He's a fine man, no... anyway, he's a man like any other. Besides, I've known him for almost a year, without really knowing him.

You'll laugh, you'll say that I shouldn't let my wife's cousins in the house. I know all too well the stories that could be told... Pgt! Let's not exaggerate. Keep in mind that my wife is always irritable, she exaggerates everything; for two years that I've been talking reasonably to her, she replies with hysterical fits. I don't want to give up on marriage. I know quite well that marriage is useful to the family. You've said everything when you've said family! What is it, the family? It's a man, a woman, and then their children, if they have children. It's not that I want to say anything bad about the family, nor about property. Property, that's owning something, having something to own, and when you own it you're a proprietor. So you can't deny property! But let's not discuss it, it would take us too far from the subject.

So then, I was holding onto my paper and my hat: then there's a rather strong gust of wind, no, let's not exaggerate, a strong gust of wind, that blows the paper from my left hand. I catch it with my right hand, but let go of my hat. The little lady starts walking faster, I try to follow her, the wind becomes stronger, it blows my hat away; to catch it, I let go of my paper, and since then I haven't seen the paper, the hat, or the little lady... Ah, yes! When I leaned over the bridge, I saw my hat going off like that (*Undulatory gesture.*) down the Seine... I was annoyed, standing bare-headed on the bridge. A kid shouted out: Oh la la!... He was exaggerating.

A passerby told me I could get my hat back from the nets, in Saint-Cloud. We have an admirable administration, no, a good administration. I'll get my hat back. Before going home, I have to go by Saint-Cloud, you know, where the nets are? (*He pulls out his watch.*) It's not late, it's not early, it's my time.

By the way, what did my wife have to say, anyway? I'll bet it's more exaggerations. (*He reads.*) "Life is impossible with you, I'm leaving with Oscar." (*Bewilderment.*) You can see how much she exaggerates! Well, some men in my situation would start shouting, crying: My wife is... Me, no, I'll run... no, I'll go look for her. I'll find her and speak reason to her. Women, men, things, everything in nature is becoming so exaggerated, I'll get my hat back, I'll get my wife back, and I'll remain reasonable! (*He exits, without hurrying.*)

*"Pgt!" is a little smacking of the lips and tongue against the lips, which expresses supreme wisdom.

AIR DE L'OBSESSION

OBSESSION

THE OBSESSIVE: M. Coquelin Cadet

(*He enters, pale and haggard.*) Ah! I'm very sick. And yet, only two days ago I was so happy! I went to the theater, to the Délassements. They had an amusing little play! Oh, so amusing! There was a young lady (in the play), and then a young man who wanted to marry the young lady, and then people who tried to prevent the marriage, and then other people who were for the marriage, anyway I don't remember very well what happens, but they get married in the end. Then everyone is happy, and they sing an air, oh! what a tune!

Tra la la la, la la, la la la, etc.

(*He sings the whole air.*)

When I left the theater I was happy; such a pretty little play. It was so cold!... I turn up my collar, I walk fast, la la, my shoes ring out on the pavement, la la, la la. I live one hour from the theater. I reach my door, I ring, bing, bing, bing, bing, bing. (*Same air.*) The doorman takes three quarters of an hour to open for me. Finally! I climb the stair (I live on the sixth floor), la, la, la, la. I light my candle, la la; I get undressed; I throw my coat on a chair, la la, my pants on another, la la; I jump into bed and go to sleep.

(*Snoring to the same air.*)

In the morning, I wake up; the weather is superb; I had a ray of sunshine up my nose.

I leap out of bed, tra, la, la, la, la; I duck my head in the water, glub, glub, glub, glub. (*Same air.*) I dry off, I knot my tie, la la; I was happy! There's a knock at the door, I go to open, la, la, la, la. My concierge! Aha, it's you? You really made me wait at the door last night, la la. What's this? A letter... Versailles. (*Gesture of opening and reading it.*) La, la, la la. Ah, my God! My poor aunt... On her deathbed...! My hat! Coat, umbrella! I'm downstairs; I catch a cab: Driver! Saint-Lazare station, five francs for a tip, la, la, la la. I get to the station; I forget my umbrella in the car, car, car, car, car. (*Same air.*) The ticket window was closing, I got my ticket anyway, there I am in the train, oof, oof, oof

(*Same air.*), the train that's leaving is the express, press, press, press, press. (*Same air.*) My poor aunt! I'm very fond of my poor aunt; even though she's my aunt by marriage. I arrive; she dies in my arms! Oh, I'm heartbroken, oken, oken, oken, oken. Oh! That air bothers me. I had to run everywhere; make a statement of death, eth, eth, eth, eth, write an obituary, ary, ary, ary, ary, that air is so irritating; it chased me even as I took her to her final resting place. The man in the hardware store said: You are very sad, monsieur?—Oh, let's not talk about it, it, it, it, it. That air is horrible. Anyway, since it won't leave me alone, I'll use it to express my sorrow. (*He sings.*)

I have just lost my dear old auntie,
And she is never coming back.
Maybe the will she left was scanty,
But I can buy a suit of black.

So she can move around at leisure,
She has a box with lots of room.
Nobody has a bit of pleasure
When you can't move around your tomb!

At last it was over. I got on the train, train, train, train, train, which whistles, which departs. My head is bursting, ting, ting, ting, ting; I arrive at the station, shun, shun, shun, shun, at Saint-Lazare, zar, zar, like a lunatic, tick, tick! Oh, that air, air, air, air, air!

I shove everyone aside, I take the street in front of the station, I turn left, I turn right, right, right, right, right, then left again; I come out at the Seine; a bridge, bridge, bridge, bridge, bridge; I get on the bridge, I look at the water, water, water, water, water. Ah, no more singing! Death! I throw myself into the river, I drown, glub, glub, glub, glub.

(*Sigh of satisfaction.*)

When I came to, I was in the rescue station for the drowned and asphyxiated. My clothes were drying by the fire. Something came back into my head; I had lost the water, but kept the air! Air, air, air, air.

(*He exits, pitiful, singing the air.*)

THE MAN WHO HAS TRAVELED

THE TRAVELER: M. Coquelin Cadet

(*He enters rubbing his hands.*)
I have my ticket; my bags are checked, including the parrot and the four washing machines I promised my friend Hernandez in the Cape Verde Islands. I have half an hour to kill; I'd just as soon spend it with you.

I arrive this morning at eleven thirty, instead of ten fifty-seven, the train was ten minutes late. I was supposed to have lunch with a close friend. (Oh1 I tidied up in the train; I'm used to it. When you know how to travel!) Me, with a seltzer bottle and a match, I take a Russian bath. So my friend William has lunch at eleven on the dot, no, not William, that's my friend in Gibraltar, but Dubois. (I was mistaken; you know how it is, always on the road.) Is it because I was late? He seemed somewhat aloof. But after that, he became friendly, and the lunch would have been charming for me, if I could see and hear certain things in peace. Me, I can't, I can't help it.

We had some sardines, some soft-boiled eggs. On the sardine can, there was the name of I don't know who in Nantes, and then the wine, it was a Burgundy. Now, my friend Dubois was born on the rue Beaubourg, he's barely left it, he's never been in Nantes, or in Burgundy, he knows nothing about them. So why did he serve those things in his home? Soft-boiled eggs are known and eaten everywhere; that's why I restrained myself, I didn't mention it; I even talked about other things, I told him about some of my travels. For example, I told him a… No, it's not a story, it's an observation: one day I was in Pomerania, no, in Herzegovina, in a little place next to Pest… so it wasn't in Herzegovina, no, I'm confused, it was in Crimea, that's it, in Crimea. I was on a road and I saw a farmer; you know, one of those people who work the earth; the earth where you plant something and it grows (you have to travel to get an idea of it). This farmer was planting cabbages; well, it was curious to see how he was planting his cabbages, he was planting them… he had a gesture… anyway, you could feel all the customs, all the local color of Sicily, no, I mean Herzegovina.

I don't know why, but as I was talking Dubois seemed nervous, irritated. That boy hasn't traveled, he hasn't acquired the flexibility of character you get from traveling. I can assure you that if I have children I'll make them travel at once and constantly without stopping. So lunch continued then, they brought a heap of things, mutton chops, I don't know what; there was pepper on the chops, the pepper was good, it's true, and I know about pepper. I was in Cayenne where they export a thousand tons of pepper a year; you should see the dock-hands sneeze!—Dubois ate his chops with a look like that, as calm as you please. It annoyed me, but anyway, I controlled myself and talked about other things. They were talking about some Venus de Milo whose arms were broken. They seemed to find it funny that I'd never seen her. Me, I've been to Milo (they've never been there), and didn't see any Venus; she's in Paris; it doesn't surprise me; me, I don't stay in Paris; I'm not a mushroom like them. And besides, this Venus, what is she? They described her to me. It's not because she has no arms; it's an accident, it's not her fault; and besides I've seen so many broken things in my travels. But what's she like, this Venus? They told me she was about two and a half meters high. (*He bursts out laughing.*) Come talk to me about some statue that's two and a half meters high, me, who's gone through the Karokoram, in the middle of Asia, where there's a statue of Buddha that's a hundred and four meters high and sixty-five meters wide! Come talk to me about sculpture now! They looked at each other; I felt it was going badly. However, Dubois did eveything nicely, they uncorked some champagne. There were two individuals at lunch speaking English, unless it was Spanish; I don't know, I have no time to learn languages; I only pass through countries. And yet it's valuable to learn a few words of foreign languages, it broadens your ideas. Like with me, before traveling I was an imbecile, an absolute imbecile. They're a curious thing, languages, but I don't know any; wait, while traveling through Tyrol, no, through the Duchy of Würzburg, I learned a word, that word... yes that's it: Strumpf (*pronounce it chtroummpf*) it means... um, uh, well, it's untranslatable, you have to have been in the country to understand it! I told them about that and plenty of other things, because you know when you travel, you have stories about it!

They brought dessert, fruit, cheese, well! from Holland: it was too strong… not Holland, but that kind of cheese. I said to Dubois: Have you been to Holland? Do you know that country with its canals, with its teapots that are so shiny; everyone sees himself in them and looks so chubby, pregnant women look in them and have chubby children, I even looked chubby myself, and say, even the cheese in Holland looks chubby! No, you don't know it? Well then, I find it improper for you to serve cheese from Holland in your home! He answered me sharply (he never traveled, it's understandable), and then they shouted, they drowned out my voice, they brought coffee, liqueurs, cigars. Coffee to me, who has crossed Arabia in every direction! I passed on the coffee, but I asked Dubois, gently, oh so gently!: Have you been to Grande Chartreuse? There was Chartreuse on the table. He answered me no. I know it well.—And these cigars? From Havana. (*Loud.*) From Havana? It's true, they're from Havana, me I can say that because I know. But you, you lie when you say they're from Havana, because you've never been to Havana. Me, I've been to Havana, I caught yellow fever there: so, you're a liar, a scoundrel, and a coward!… Yes, I said a coward, I couldn't control myself; I was harsh, but I was just. You see, when you've traveled, your blood moves easily, your blood travels. He looked astonished. I threw a glass of kirsch in his face, the way they do in Valladolid, no I'm sorry in Scutari! He grew pale, got up, and me I ran for my hat, while he kicked me in the butt (you know, like the Scots do). He sent two individuals after me—his seconds—people who had never been to America! I wrapped myself in my dignity, and arranged a meeting for right here at fifty-three minutes past midnight to duel in the night (like the Patagonians); but I'm catching a train at eleven forty-nine (that's a Persian duel); it's eleven forty-four; I'm on my way.

(*He leaves.*)

THE MAN WHO WAS A SUCCESS

THE SUCCESSFUL MAN: M. Coquelin Cadet

(*Evening dress. He enters fanning himself with his flat hat.*)
She's ravishing, that baroness, but she's exhausting. In vain have I cried out everywhere that I can't waltz, I don't know what's wrong with all the ladies; they've arranged things so well, that in a moment I'll have to begin again with the marquise. Oh, women! They're charming, but they don't follow through on their ideas.

And how could I avoid waltzing? Me, an attaché to the ambassador, first class attaché since this morning. But the waltz shakes me, distracts me, I lose the thread of my idea.

Anyway, we're alone, we can talk. I was born in Le Mans, but I wasn't raised in Le Mans; it was in a little place near Le Mans that I was raised, I learned about writing from the woman in the post office. My father knows her, she had little receptions on Saturday, you know, lotto, hot water.

Well, it was there that I started to become ambitious.

On Sunday, in the afternoon, I went to the Hotel du Commerce to relax, to hear people talk, to get the news. There was a cook dressed in white, whose name was Martin. He struck up a friendship with me, this Martin, he thought I looked like his mother. It's from him I got my idea, and with him that I studied. Oh! I'm not a cook, because I'm an attaché to the ambassador, first class since this morning.

(*He listens.*) I have time, they're starting the quadrille.—yes, this Martin made pommes soufflées, my God, not extraordinarily, but, in short, he made them. Me, I watched him, and said:—How do you get them to puff up like that? You'd think they had air in them. He said to me:—It's very simple: (Oh, he wasn't very good) I let the fat cool down… Anyway, he explained his technique.

At first, he made fun of me, this Martin, then he seemed angry, I made them better than he did, those pommes soufflées. We quarreled, and I didn't keep going to the hotel, because I don't like to spend my time with cooks. But I made pommes soufflées myself (Iff!).

I remember the first time I tried, I was at papa's house; at first it surprised him, I hadn't told him, and mama came crying; "I don't want you staying in the kitchen like that." So I just laughed and locked the door. I made my plate of pommes soufflées. My father is an excellent man, but he doesn't know... anyway, my plate was a sensation!... You know how it is in the provinces!

It was there, there was that tax collector who talked about it in the sub-prefecture and said: "He's an impossible boy!" You don't believe it? Well! I was invited to the sub-prefecture. And it was there that the tax collector's wife was being treated for a chill by a doctor whose sister... anyway it would take too long to tell you. Anyone but me would have been intimidated. Me, no, I had my idea. I looked at the chimney. I always look at the chimney first when I enter a living room. At half past midnight everyone was going to bed (it was a small sub-prefecture), the tax collector's wife says to me: "Do something funny, you're so funny, everyone's leaving." So me I tell some big lout of a servant in short pants and white legs, he was carrying a platter with syrups. I start shouting:—Bring me a towel, a frying pan, and some lard. Everyone stops chatting. I heard ladies say behind their fans: "Oh, he's so funny! What's he going to do?" Then the sub-prefect starts clapping and saying: "That's it, a towel." And me I add: "And some gray salt and some potatoes and a knife, no, no, I have my own knife." So they bring me that, I install myself before the fire, I remove the fire-guards, I rub the pan with a packet of letters I had in my pocket, I keep my gloves on; I always keep my gloves on. I put the pan on the fire, the lard in the pan. I give the pan to the sub-prefect's cousin, a very nice boy (oh, he was quite useful to me!) but he won't get far in administration; he doesn't follow through on his ideas.—So me, I install myself with the towel on my knees (my pants were covered with lint; they have bad linen in sub-prefectures). I peel the potatoes into the towel, so as not to get my gloves dirty, I always cut them into the towel, I keep the peelings in a corner of the towel, and then, the cut potatoes, bang! I let them fall into the hot fat. (*He listens.*) Oh! I still have time, they're only at the third figure of the quadrille. Then the potatoes were in the hot fat. I watch them, they start to cook. They have to be pale, very pale; I take them from the fire—and I say: "No, they're ruined, they're ruined, a polka!"

Some of the people there made such faces! My future was at stake, I had to succeed. When the polka was over, I put the potatoes back on the fire. I had put in very few potatoes (it has to be very few), then the first one puffs up, and then the other pieces, all of them, it was like a trail of gunpowder, they swelled up, they rose. I was saved. I make a gesture as I move the pan, I turn around: there were a good twenty-five people behind me. I cry: The salt! The salt! Everyone runs to look for the salt. I salt the first piece (after draining it). "Madame sub-prefect, please do me the honor." Listen, you could see light through those potatoes; it was nothing but air. It was a sensation! I was launched completely. It was following that evening that I came to Paris. (*He listens.*) I hear the waltz, no, it's the galop of the quadrille. I was launched, and despite all my enemies, since then I've had nothing but success, success... And yet one time, come to think of it, it was with the Prince Chikekski (a Pole), at the Chateau des Pressoirs. Well, I came close to losing my position. There were a lot of guests there, artists, scholars, military, you know, all those people who don't follow through on their ideas; they didn't succeed.

I had been at the castle for a week, I say to myself: "The moment has come." I looked sad, as usual, because I don't like small talk, I never chat, you understand with my reputation. The ladies were saying: "What's the matter with him? He's in love, he who's so funny... they say he's been staring at Madame So-and-So." It's not true, I never stare because I'm following my idea. So then, there were a lot of people there, a general with two staff officers, some young people... (Oh, those salon jealousies), it was the right moment, I begin: Complete success, they puffed up like that. (*Gesture.*) Like balloons, it worked so well that my word, I allowed myself a liberty, an innovation; I asked three young ladies to make me paper cones, lots of paper cones. I remove the pan, I take the potatoes, I put one of them in each paper cone, because there weren't many pieces, I had counted them, all the ladies had one and I throw them (*Gesture.*) like that. They fall on the ladies, on their fans, on their shoulders, it was a success!... Unfortunately, I make a wrong move, one of the cones lands in the general's eye, the cone opens, the potato falls in his boots, he sneezes, he rubs his eye; one of the young men in the staff comes up to me, I don't remember what he said, anyway it was a scandal. I don't like duels, I wouldn't fight for anything in the world, except for my idea. Oh no, I don't like duels, I'm not a soldier, not at all; and then on the grounds, I was in such a state! I didn't know where I was. It was no fun! And besides I don't know a word of fencing, I never studied it. They put a sword in my hand, my head spins, I think I'm holding the handle of a pan, I turn, I do that, he comes toward me. I don't know how it happens, I killed him; the seconds claimed they weren't familiar with the thrust. So I came close to being prosecuted, but they hushed up the affair and sent me as a third class attaché to Birmingham. What did I do in Birmingham? Always the same thing. When you have an idea, you have to follow it. I made pommes soufflées. Favorable report to the Minister of Foreign Affairs, second report very flattering. There were lords who came; they were very pleased, those lords.

But there's the wife of a big manufacturer of razors (they make millions of pounds sterling in that house)... Anyway, that woman made a fuss over me. So they appointed me second class in Japan. And in Japan? I made pommes soufflées; they called me back here, and now I'm first class. The waltz is starting. (*False exit.*) Have an idea and follow it. I'll explain to you how to make pommes soufflées... but it won't do you any good, it's old hat now. (Ah, that waltz!) I don't have time... one last word of advice... get your own idea and follow it, (Marquise, I'm all yours!) and you'll be a success.

THE MAN WITH HIS FEET TURNED AROUND

Fine! I'll wait.—Oh, those office boys!—I'm here to get my name corrected, because I got a medal...—Hey! I don't have my medal!... I forgot it.—Never mind, I'll go to the shop across the street, and buy another one.—Yes, I got a medal, under someone else's name; you can read about it in the *Official*: "Captain Wacky, for exceptional service, etc...."—Oh, it's quite a story.

I had a little room, on rue Beaubourg, on the eighth floor—a very pretty little room, but a bit small.—I worked for a company that sold insurance against undertakers. Salary: 1100 francs a year.—I always kept my boots with the heels under the bed and the toes toward the window,—because I have regular habits, very regular.—I get up every morning at five. In my company, they only want serious workers; I have to be there at seven o'clock sharp, and it takes a good hour and a quarter to get to the office. It's right at the top of La Chapelle.—One evening (this was about a year ago), I don't know what came over me. I was in a lively mood; I had met a little lady on my way back from the office. Oh, I didn't follow her: you know, 1100 francs a year! But going up to my room, I hit my head on the stairway. My head was spinning; I don't know how I got my boots off; and I put them, without thinking, with the toes under the bed and the heels toward the window! So the next morning (it was so cold!), at five o'clock sharp, I jump out of bed (no, I didn't jump, the ceiling was too low), I get out of bed, I open the snuffbox (the window, I mean! I don't take snuff, I sneeze, but that's because of the draft).—I open the window, then, to wake myself up (it was so cold!), I take my boots (it was so dark!). I put on my boots. They hurt! I say to myself: it must be my corns, it's so cold. I pull on my boots: they hurt so much! (I'll cut my corns tomorrow). They hurt terribly! But the office won't wait. I pull harder, and finally I get my boots on (but oh, how they hurt!). Six o'clock! I'm running late. I get my hat, I don't put it on, because I'd break the window if I did. I open the door. Bang! I fall downstairs. Oh! I must have rolled down ten steps.

No, it's impossible! My corns hurt too much. I try to head back to my room, but instead of going upstairs, I go downstairs. It's bizarre, there I am in the street. Well! When I hit my head the night before, I twisted my neck, and even my shoulders hurt; I can't hold my arms straight. It's very irritating. Finally, after a few attempts, I get my head almost turned around. I was late; I'd been walking all that time. Where was I? I'd gone in the opposite direction from my office! It's bizarre.

A railway station. The circuit line; I had twelve sous on me. I'll sacrifice them; it'll take me back to La Chapelle. I buy a ticket; there were two trains; I run for the train to La Chapelle, and fall into the other one. Going the other way!

At Saint-Lazare station, I want to get off. A man shouts: "All aboard for the express!" The express is not for me; I'm going to La Chapelle. I run for the train for La Chapelle, and fall into the express, which lets out a whistle and leaves.

I wasn't alone in my compartment. There was a lady. That was annoying; otherwise I could have taken off my boots, which hurt so much! But really, I don't mind; there's nothing I wouldn't do for the ladies.

Corns and a stiff neck are both painful, and, believe it or not, even make it hard to sit down. Impossible to fold myself into the seat. I finally settle down somewhat, and take a look at the lady. She was very nice, that lady. She had her face buried in her handkerchief, and I heard her going "Hee hee hee!" I thought she was crying. I'm very discreet: I tried to move away from her, and, I don't know how, ended up beside her. She began again even louder: "Hee hee hee!" But she wasn't crying at all, she was laughing; she was doubled over! I thought it was because of me; I like to amuse the ladies, and she was so nice to laugh like that!... I say to her, "You're in a cheerful mood, madame, in this fine weather." She doesn't answer me, but keeps up her "Hee hee hee!" As for me, I'd be cheerful too, except that I'm late for work, and I'm having trouble with... I was going to say "my corns," but it's not very chivalrous to talk about your corns.

All this time, the train kept going, and so fast... She finally calmed down, and we chatted (I chat well with the ladies), but my stiff neck was bothering me. It doesn't matter, I fell madly in love with her; I took her hands; I wanted to kiss them. Impossible, with my stiff neck!

I tried to fall to my knees before her; instead, I end up in her lap.

She just kept saying, "Oh, those feet, those feet! Hee hee hee!" We arrive at Le Havre; I coldly take my leave; I don't like to be ridiculed. And, besides, I was quite annoyed; I came from Paris, I was in Le Havre, and I only had a ticket for La Chapelle, near Pantin. I get off the train, I want to explain myself to the stationmaster; his office is over there; I run to it; I find myself leaving the station by a grade crossing, and then catch sight of the sea. Oh, I detest the sea! I hate water, and there's so much water in the sea. I run toward the town; the sea keeps getting closer. Horrors! There must be a flood! And that town over there trying to escape it. I run faster after the town. Splash! I fall into the sea...

Fortunately I took swimming lessons in the Saint-Martin canal; that's why I don't like water... I swim vigorously toward the shore; my boots and corns hurt so much in that cold water! Well, the shore keeps getting farther away; I swim harder, and end up in the middle of the ocean; I can't take off my boots in the water (some people can). I was lost. All of a sudden, a life preserver, you know, one of those big rings, hit me on the head; I took quite a drink then! But I hung onto it, I felt myself being hoisted up, I was on the *India Pale Ale*, a large ship belonging to the Johnson Company in Liverpohol (I can't pronounce those English words), headed for the Fiji Islands with a cargo of lozenges (it seems they catch a lot of colds over there).

They were doing a lot of work on the boat; me, I try to get out of the way so I won't disturb them, bang, I end up between the legs of the second mate, and I see the captain, who looked furious. He was on my right, or my left, I don't remember; I run off the other way, and fall into his arms. My head hits him on the nose. He starts bleeding! Blood! Mutiny! Rebellion! Two months in irons; that's how long the trip is.

Not only that, but they clamp the irons over my boots, so I can't take them off (the boots, I mean), and my corns still hurt so much! Finally, I hear cries; "Aou! Aou! Aou!" Land had been sighted; I never learned English; I was down in the hold; they pulled me out and put me ashore, in Honolulu, and the *India Pale Ale* went on to the Fiji Islands. The authorities question me. I tell them I'm an office worker, and I'm late for my job. The authorities burst out laughing, calling me "Mr. Worker." Bang! Boom! Gunshots! What is it? A native uprising. I turn pale; I run toward the port; the port was here; the natives were there. I fall right in the middle of the natives; the marines follow me; the natives point at my feet, like this, shouting, "Wacky! Wacky!" That's how they say "worker." They throw their bows, their arrows, their scalping knives, and run away. I run away too, in the opposite direction; I end up among the natives again (Oh, my corns were hurting!). The marines were right behind me. Bang! Boom! They kill all the natives, the marines make me a captain, they carry me in triumph to Honolulu, and the governor gives me a medal under the name of Captain Wacky; I try to correct him, but I don't have the strength, I pass out. You know, because of my corns...

When I came to, I was in Paris at the Orléans station; they ask me where I live; I mutter weakly "29 rue Beaubourg, eighth floor..." The room was rented to someone else. They take me to the Grand Hotel; the boy asks, "What can I do for you, monsieur?" I show him my feet. The boy slaps his forehead, leaves, and returns with my savior. He was a podiatrist. A man of genius, the first to come up with the simple, yet sublime, idea of taking off my boots! He was the one who noticed my boots were on backwards, the toes behind, the heels in front, which explained why my feet were turned around, and took me everywhere I didn't want to go!—I ran to my office! I was a year and a day late; I'd been replaced. Fortunately, I found a position in the White Rabbit department store. They like to have men with medals to direct the customers.—I came here to correct my nomination, because my name isn't Wacky, it's... Well, I don't remember; you know, being backwards for so long confuses you. Well then, I'll keep Wacky... No, that's more suitable for Honolulu. Maybe I'll change it to Walker, that's better for my new position. (*Exiting.*) Ah, it's my turn! I'm on my way!

THE LOST MAN

An elegant living room in the lost man's home.

THE SAVIOR

(*He cries out disagreeably, to no servant in particular.*)—Jean isn't here? Fine, I'll wait.

(*Alone.*)

—Always out! But I don't have time; I have to take my clothes back to the rental place. Always out! He's a lost boy!

I knew him when he was young. He's from my village. That doesn't flatter me.

To begin with, in school, he worked like an idiot; he tried to win prizes, they gave them to him... to keep him quiet. Me, I'm active; I left school after seventh grade, partly to avoid his company, because I could already tell... Anyway, let's move on. As for him, he stayed to the end, despite my advice. He must have been so stupid by the time he left!...

I was in business at the time. I was a sales clerk at the White Rabbit department store, in the ties section. I had to move, but I had no furniture, and no place to put the furniture I didn't have. I was active; I entrust some merchandise (ties are portable) to a lad named... never mind, it wasn't his real name; he was a crook, but I didn't realize it. He was supposed to bring me enough to set me up; I'd given him at least ten times the worth of the loan in merchandise. And then? You may not believe it, but I didn't make a sou from the affair, I never saw him or the ties again! And in the store, they made such a fuss over it! I was denounced, arrested, I wrote to Jean's mother. She was a rather pretty woman, she went to talk to the judge; in short, she settled the business with money, or otherwise; anyway, let's move on.

I still had to resign from business.

It was then that I saw Jean, who had just graduated, and who began doing one stupid thing after another, to put it frankly: he studied law;

he was admitted to the bar (imagine him as a lawyer!); he fell in love
with a woman, for good, and with only one woman!

(*He bursts out laughing.*)

He was spending money on that woman. So, for his sake, I bor-
rowed a rather large sum; at least that much was saved.

There was another individual courting that woman. Jean came to
see me, blubbering like a calf. He had a duel with the individual, he
fought with a sword, like a coward. He was wounded, like a coward.
I'm surprised he wasn't killed.

All of that put Jean in a bad light; wounded for a woman! He was
a lost boy!

It was then that I left him. With the money he'd loaned me (I'm active, myself), I founded an information service, investigating people's
morality. The profits were considerable, including what I earned from
the police (you know, on rue de Jérusalem) for the notes I furnished
them about my clients and acquaintances, especially Jean; a boy like
that needs to be watched.

Well then, along comes some butcher and has my furniture seized!
My files were sold as scrap; my office burned. And, to cap it all, the
police dismissed me, saying my information wasn't new enough! The
imbeciles! They want novelty! It's the sickness of the age.

And it's all Jean's fault! If he'd only loaned me a serious amount…
but he doesn't understand anything.

The year of the war, we met again (it was rather disagreeable for me:
friends like that!…) in a mobile battalion. I was in the supply corps.
Him, I don't know what he was.

One time, you know what he does, that fool Jean? He takes four
or five individuals in the battalion, people I didn't know, thank God!
And then he goes out, during the night, like a thief, around some kind
of building a good kilometer away from the outposts. You hear bing!
bang! Gunshots in the middle of the night. It wakes up a lot of fine
people who were sleeping peacefully. And then, you see Jean coming
back with his boys (one was missing) and with five Bavarians all glaring
at him, who seemed to despise him! The Bavarians were quickly locked
up. It was a bad business for Jean; he had left the camp (a mobile guard
isn't supposed to move from his position); he could have been shot.

They were weak; they decorated him, to hush up the scandal. He took it seriously; he's a lost boy!

At that time, I had just concluded an excellent affair with pots of melted butter I'd bought on approval, with no down payment. And since the supplier who sold them to me was killed, I didn't pay anything, and I resold the melted butter (it was bad, but it was still butter!) for provisions. I did my part, to save my fellow citizens from hunger; I made a very good profit. But me, I wasn't decorated!

Since the war, Jean and I, we've been on friendly terms. I ran into him everywhere, at the theater, by the sea. Only, he was seeing the kind of people I didn't care for: people who are known, who like to be seen. He too had a weakness for being seen, probably to show off his red ribbon.

During that time, the money from the melted butter melted, so to speak, and I had nothing to do, me who's so active. I went to see Jean. You know what he was busy with?... He was writing plays!...

I was without a sou; I tell him that. This is what he tells me: You always come to me to borrow money, and large sums, without warning. Well, I'd rather give you so much a month. You're active, you can always make your bad deals, but you can always fall back on that.

Can you imagine that creature lecturing me? And just because he gives me a little to scrape by on! He should have just shut up and advanced me the capital for that miserable income. But he doesn't understand anything. What a cretin!

Besides, you won't believe it, but he carried his plays around to the theaters! I remember that one or two of them were produced. He gave me a ticket for the opening night; the audience laughed all through it. He called it a comedy. Oh yes, it was a real comedy! They applauded, they applauded! You should have seen the faces of the people applauding. They were making fun of him. It made such a fuss that they performed it two hundred times; it became fashionable to go laugh at his play; he became a public target. He even went so far as to let his photo be sold in tobacco shops! Let your portrait be sold to passersby, exhibit yourself like that! I'd never do that. Nobody sells my photo! He's a lost boy!

Me, I didn't go to the wedding; what he gave me every month, you understand, it was nothing. I had to rent clothes to go see his plays, and I didn't pay for the rental. I went into debt because of him. Well, it was one night in fact, while coming back from the clothing shop, I was rather badly dressed, I went down the rue aux Ours; I see a man disguised as a dandy come toward me. He attacks me, or I think he attacks me; I defend myself, and I knock him out. The police come; they find two watches in my pocket, one in aluminum that didn't work (it was mine) and another in gold with the dandy's monogram on it. Can you see the trick to get me in trouble?

Jean defended me. I was acquitted, it's true; but I wasn't awarded any damages! He's incompetent, Jean, he's a lost boy!

And yet he had the nerve to present himself the next day at the Academy. He had called on the forty members at home, and spouted such platitudes they elected him to get rid of him. I was at his reception, he had green things on his suit. Can you imagine showing yourself in public like that, disguised as a parrot! Ah, he's done for!

But I'm starting to get impatient waiting for him like this. At five o'clock, I have to return my suit to the shop. Jean is so stupid that I have to get dressed up to come see him. Oh yes! He irritates me. He's completely lost. I can't do anything more for him, and I'll never set foot here again... (*He goes away and returns.*) except to collect my money. (*He leaves, furious.*)

THE GREEN DAY

THE GREEN MAN: M. Galipaux

(*He enters holding a little comb and mirror set. He looks at himself.*)

No, this evening it doesn't show. (*To the audience.*) It doesn't show, does it? What? What doesn't show? Ah! It's true. I haven't told you what happened to me.

First of all, I have a job, a job at… No sense telling you where, you'd just go chatter to the administration. At any rate, I have a job, always working, always sitting, never a vacation. So, last Saturday, Oscar (he's in the same office as me), Oscar says: "We can't go on like this; if you like, tomorrow we'll go to the country. Oh! The country!" Oscar said that flaring his nostrils; his nostrils are very big. "So, tomorrow morning, without fail, at eight o'clock, at…" I won't mention the station, you'd just go chatter to the administration. The next day, at seven o'clock, I jumped out of bed. It was a beautiful day (it was a cold day). Let's go! Everything's fine; oh! There's air, there's greenery, run, jump, dance, sing, tra la la, a light suit, my panama, and I'm off!

At the station, I see Oscar and his wife. They looked so funny! Oscar had a green veil, in the English style, and his wife a green shawl (not a pretty green, however). I join them; Oscar jumps on me, he pins a green veil to my Panama (it's very good for the sun and the dust). He's very fond of me, that Oscar.

"Green peas! Green peas!" What's that? It seemed to be coming from Madame Oscar. I jump into the air; a gust of wind lifts the green shawl; I see a nasty beak—a parrot's. It's Cocotte. We brought her because if we left her alone at home, she'd fire us… scratch, Cocotte, scratch. She can also say fine arrrtichokes; she learned that last year, her cage was in the window, and lots of peddlers went by! Say: "Fine arrrtichokes!" But the bird would only say "Green peas"!

We go into a snack shop to have a bite. They're sweeping up, the chairs are on the table. A waiter, with messy hair, dirty hands, in a dark apron, comes up to us:

—Lady and gentlemen, out in the grove there, you'll be better.

—That's it, out in the grove (*Gesture of applause.*), says Madame Oscar.

The grove is a narrow courtyard, with walls as high as that... and more walls, only three of them; the fourth is a boiler for a washhouse. It was so cold!... We were dressed very lightly. There was a wooden trellis, without the ghost of a plant, a wooden table (the water from the pump flowed under it, also on my feet!...), wooden benches, and all of it slathered with green paint, including the three walls as high as that, the boiler for the washhouse, and even the pump.

They brought us veal that had been soaked in sorrel, watercress, and white wine (that is to say, vinegar). We had to empty the bottle. Cocotte never stopped squawking "Green peas!" I looked for some parsley to give her, but there wasn't any... Thirteen and a half francs! It was me who paid, Oscar went to get the tickets.

The train was about to leave, when the horrible parrot betrays herself with her cry; the conductor won't let us through. He wants to put the parrot in the dog section. Oscar gets angry:

"Hey, conductor, be polite to my wife!"

The train leaves during the argument. We go to the stationmaster, who allows the parrot on the next train, in an hour. An hour in the station, with cold feet, with watercress and white wine in your belly, facing an enormous poster for the "Beautiful Garden" (a department store), a poster in a bright green that hurts your eyes!... And the nasty fowl cried without stopping: "Green peas!"

"Passengers for the circle line, all aboard!"

We get up. Oscar looked pale, it was the white wine... Or else the English veil on his derby. I had such a headache! I was smoking a cigar made from cabbage leaves, bought from the newsstand in the waiting room. I felt sick... was it the watercress or the cigar?

—Circle line, circle line.

We get off the train. Oscar asks:—The train for?... (it's a place he knows).

—It just left.—And the next?—In two hours.

—Oh! Well, let's go by foot; we could use a walk; I know the area, says Oscar.

I don't trust people who know the area; they're always wrong.

We followed an interminable road, between two walls, sharp cobblestones. The sky was overcast. I had stomach pains. Oh! That white wine!… The sky was looking worse. Well, good! Some rain… maybe that will get rid of my headache. Oscar was getting on my nerves.

—How fresh the air is! In a short half hour, we'll reach papa Lamèche, at the end of the street. You know the place, a house with green shutters?

I didn't know the place, but I did have a headache. The bird clinging to Madame Oscar's shoulder never stopped screeching.

—Darling, couldn't you get Cocotte to keep quiet a bit?

—My dear, you know how the fresh air excites her. You should have told me not to bring her, then, or to stay at home with her. You're always like this, in the country…

Then it began to rain seriously. Nothing but walls. Where could we find shelter?

At last, there we were at papa Lamèche, as soaked as three soups, or four counting the parrot.

—Let's drink something strong, that'll dry us out, says Oscar.

We had some absinthe, we played billiards, you know, with square balls and rough cues. The rain didn't stop. Oscar was witty; it was horrible. My headache was joined by a sore throat. We had dinner there. I could no longer see straight. I vaguely remember a sorrel soup, a spinach omelet, and salad, lots of salad. And then… yes, that's it, we came back to the station; it was raining even harder than before. The car smelled like a wet dog. It turned my stomach. At Paris, they put me in an open car; that's the only kind to have when it's raining.

Oscar gives my address: coachman, green lantern, here's your neighborhood.

I thought I was saved; in Paris, no more country, no more greenery! Horrors! The car followed the boulevard Haussmann. All those trees to the left and the right… I thought I'd die.

When I came to, I was in my bed, a prince of science, a nurse, a sister of charity surrounded me. The sister puts her hand over my mouth to keep me from speaking. I resist, I jump out of bed. At the wardrobe mirror, I recoil at my reflection. I was as green as pea soup. I'd caught jaundice!

I'm cured, today, or mostly. (*Pulling out his comb and mirror set.*) It doesn't show anymore, does it? It doesn't matter, you can't make me go running around in the woods again.

THE FRIEND OF THE FAMILY

THE FRIEND: F. Galipaux

(*He enters indignant.*) No, never again shall I set foot in their house! What do you expect? Ingratitude, now that really gets my goat.

That miserable Oscar!... No, I can't even mention him without losing my temper. And yet I'm not a bad sort...

(*He softens, and sniffles.*) Not at all a bad sort; first of all, friendship, for me, is sacred. I was Oscar's friend!... Well, you'll see what he did to me, that Oscar. I'd known him for two years, had seen him every day without fail, even on holidays. I arrived at his place early in the morning, around ten o'clock. He's married, Oscar is; that's stupid on his part (but with a friend, I'm very tolerant). And he has children; which is even more stupid. It took all my friendship to... well, let's move on!

Yes, he has two children! One of each sex! They run around, they jabber all the time, it's irritating, the little one especially, even though he looks like his mother (Oh! Iff!), a very pretty woman, but really, a fine type of woman! It was the height of stupidity for Oscar to marry a pretty woman—I mean a woman who's superb, and cute!

Oh, yes! Absolute stupidity! But it's all the same to me: with friends, I'm very tolerant, he only has himself to blame. And besides it was a treat to the eye to see Madame Oscar coming and going, like that, in the apartment. Oh, the ingrate! Well, let's move on!

I arrived then around ten o'clock; I lived next to them. Oscar worked at some job, I don't know what; he scribbled on paper. I let him do it; me, I drank white wine. It cleans the stomach, in the morning. And Oscar has white wine (plapp)! Oh, the ingrate!

But the children were there! And I who need peace and quiet, before lunch! Well! Last winter, with how cold it was, and there's always a good fire at Oscar's, a huge fire (he's so wasteful); the children came to get warm, and then the maid... She's very nice, that maid; that was stupid too—not for Oscar, but his wife; furthermore, I didn't say anything when they hired her, and besides, it's a treat to the eye to see a little maid... Anyway, let's move on!

So, the maid was washing the kids' snotty little faces with a sponge and warm water, right in front of the fire! Me, when I want to get warm, I don't like a bunch of people blocking the heat, especially kids. And so I said to the maid: "When I was their age, it used to get very cold, much colder than today. To wash myself? I used to go out in the courtyard, I broke the ice on the pump. To get warm? Never by the fire! I used to go out and rub my hands with snow. That's what keeps you warm!" (It's not true, but it's good to say in front of children.) The little ones stared at me with big eyes, and then went to play in a corner. Poor kids! I felt sorry for them—but they're as strong as Turks: they owe their health to me.

You have to be strict with children, especially if you want any peace and quiet.

Well! At lunch or dinner, the little ones always wanted sauce with their meat. I told them: "At your age, I ate nothing but beans, every day, nothing but beans. Sauce makes you grow old." It's a joke; it's amusing at mealtime. The children don't understand it, but it improves their minds. And I held out my plate to Madame Oscar: "So give me some sauce!" Madame Oscar looked at me coldly;—but it was just to avoid suspicion;—in front of her husband, you understand! He also looked coldly at me, because he sensed danger. And he was right; it's bound to happen to him... Just think! Such a pretty woman! I too sensed danger and wanted to prevent it. A friend must be warned—especially about things like that.

I was often alone with Oscar,—in the evening, when I returned from my walk after dinner. It's very good to take a walk after dinner; and my goodness! Despite my friendship for them (you can't insist that a friend be in your home, always, always!), I used to go out for a little fresh air. One evening, I return; my digestion was in fine fettle. Madame Oscar had gone to bed (a headache). She often has, or *claims* to have, a headache when I'm there;—it's probably her husband that bothers her. Oscar was yawning, yawning. He sensed danger. So, I wanted to give him a little advice;—advice from a friend.

Between two glasses of beer (they have excellent brown beer; it helps my digestion, in the evening. Oh, the ingrate!), I begin bluntly by saying: "I can guess what's bothering you. Your wife... so young... as pretty as she is...you're afraid..." "Afraid of what?" He looked like he didn't understand (he's stubborn).

"It's bound to happen, you know it, I know it; you can expect it. Take some advice from a friend: don't worry about it... Why work yourself up about it? Say! Your maid isn't bad; she's very nice, that maid of yours. I'm very tolerant, I won't tell anyone. It'll distract you."

Then he says to me with a stupid look on his face: "I don't like that kind of joke." He told me good night. It wasn't even twenty-five after midnight! The ingrate!

Too bad for him if he won't understand. Oh! He's stubborn! And then his wife will trick him into... eating tin scraps as macaroni. And both of them became colder and colder with me. Madame Oscar? It was all a ruse. Oh! Women! And so, she often served mashed potatoes with chops. Oscar likes mashed potatoes; I don't; I've often told her... But I realized that she had to avoid suspicion, and so I didn't mention it anymore. That life lasted another six months!

Poor Oscar! He yawned more and more, his wife had more and more headaches;—it couldn't go on like that. There had to be a change, a basic change in their way of life. So, I came up with a plan, this is what I suggested to Oscar just today, I said to him:

"First of all, you send your children to boarding school. They're too young! I'll find some boarding school that will take them young. It's important, because they mustn't see what will happen; because you know very well (don't act stupid!) you know what will happen, for certain. Your wife, so young, such a pretty woman..."

He tried to interrupt me, but I was determined to accomplish my duty as a friend, fully, and I continued:

(*Very quickly.*) "Be quiet! Danger is imminent. Strangers could come here; me, I'm always in the house; I'm your friend; I'm discreet; no one will know a thing. I'll take care of the matter; you'll be at ease; so will your wife. Besides, the maid... (Iff!) That will distract you..."

Oscar got to his feet. He looked happy. I thought he understood my plan... not at all! He placed his two hands on my shoulders; he looked me in the eye; he pushed with one hand and pulled with the other; that spun me around, and... (*gesture of being kicked*), I shall never set foot in their house again!

(*He leaves with dignity.*)

THE CLEAN MAN

Monologue

Performed by Coquelin Cadet, of the Comédie-Française.

(*He enters flicking dust from the sleeves and trimmings of his suit.*)

I haven't eaten, because I stupidly accepted a dinner invitation from Oscar.

Oh! I never eat in town: I suffer too much, but the Marquise des Platesbandes and her daughter were dining with Oscar. The other day, I got into the marquise's good graces by giving her the recipe for a dandruff shampoo that's a tradition in my family.

So I say to Oscar: "She's charming, that Mademoiselle des Platesbandes." And so then he organizes this fancy dinner for tonight. He's a smart boy, apparently, Oscar, but he's not... He doesn't have the habit... the religion! of cleanliness. Me, I may not have an extraordinary imagination, but at least I'm clean!

This morning, I wake up. I think: dinner at Oscar's! Well!

I take my bath. Like every day, I have my hour of pedicure, my hour of manicure, and I spend a half hour on my hair. And I have breakfast.

Four boiled eggs: I like them, because nobody can touch eggs inside. I eat bread made by machine... Nobody touches the dough: when it leaves the oven, they put it in a napkin and bring it to me. I drink filtered water at my table; a little filter, an excellent system... (I'll give you the address of the manufacturer.)

After breakfast, I wash my hands, I wash my face, I change my linen, I put on fresh shoes, I wash my hands again, and I go out. I go to Auguste to have my hair brushed: you know, shampooed.

I get a shampoo every day, from three to four.

It gives you an appetite, a shampoo, when you've had nothing but boiled eggs. So I return home; I wash my hands, I wash my face... (The dust on the way back...) I change my linen, I change my clothes, I put on fresh shoes, I wash my hands again, and I go out. At Auguste's, I get a last touch-up with the comb, and I'm on my way! To Oscar's! Because the dinner was for six o'clock.

"Good evening Madame, good evening Oscar, good evening Marquise, good evening Mademoiselle, good evening everyone." I excuse myself to wash my hands… (The dust…)

In the soup I find a fresh little carrot… (I'm rather fond of carrots…) peeled by hand! (The cook's hand!)

At my house, vegetables are peeled by machine, turned like this… (I'll give you the name of the manufacturer.)

(*With conviction.*) I don't touch the soup!… They pass the bread, cut by hand, on a plate. I don't say a thing! I take a slice; I drop it in my napkin, which is clean, it's true. (It was the only clean thing on the table.—Oh yes! The tablecloth and knives also looked clean.) I cut a little slice from the top of the bread, a little slice from the bottom, and peel away the crust around it. That way, I had a little nugget of bread that was clean enough. (It was bread made by machine, as I'd requested.)

Oscar seemed to notice my little task, and started to look annoyed.

Well! I didn't eat anything but that little piece of bread. Everything they served reminded me of the cook, who had tied the sirloin, trussed the turkey, shelled the beans!

It made me sick to my stomach, just seeing the others eat all that stuff.

I only drank a little Bordeaux, because they make it cleanly enough. In Bordeaux, they don't trample the grapes like that. (*Demonstrates with his feet.*) They do it by machine…

With every full plate set before me, Oscar became more and more unhappy: he could tell none of it was clean…

Oh! I was so patient! But when I saw the marquise and her daughter (her daughter!) eating wild strawberries without washing them, strawberries picked in the woods! (They're not clean, those woods…) and picked by hand (They're not clean, those hands…), when I saw that, I arose from the table, I exploded, I told Oscar:

"No! You're not clean, nothing in your house is clean, not even the guests!"

Oscar grew pale, stood up, showed me the door, while the marquise gave her daughter a bottle to sniff, saying: "You were right! The man has no manners whatsoever."

I shrugged my shoulders, I left the room. I asked for some soap to wash my hands, but Oscar followed me; he threw my coat over my head, and tossed my hat onto the landing. The door shut, and... (*A pause, several grimaces.*)

But what's wrong with me? Ah! It's my stomach... I'm leaving. I have to go back home to change my shoes, wash my hands, and eat...

Eat what, at this hour? Oh, bah! Four more boiled eggs. At least nobody touches them inside. Oh, you know, if I'm leaving now, it's really not because I'm hungry, but... (*He flicks dust from his suit.*) frankly, it's not clean here! Good night.

THE HANGED MAN

(*He seizes his neck with a grimace.*)

Pay no attention!—It's just a tic, a gesture that's stayed with me since that whole business.

What business? Ah, that's right! I haven't told you I was hanged. Yes, hanged… It's due to the fact that I never had any luck.

Well, when I was young, they gave me bread with jam or bread with butter—depending on the time of day.—Well then! I always dropped my bread on the floor, and it always fell on the wrong side, or rather the right side (the side with the butter or jam), and the floor was always dusty! All of that shows my bad luck. (*Tic.*)

And then? It continued. At school, I was promised third prize in gymnastics. (I never won a prize.)

To practice for the test, one night, I left the dormitory, I slid down a drainpipe into the gymnasium, and I started working on the trapeze. I try to do a flip, bang, I fall on my belly (like my bread). I cry out, the watchman comes in and takes me back to my bed. I had two weeks of colic and three hundred lines to write every day in my… (*he rubs his belly*) quiet moments. As for the prize, you understand? After that escapade, pst. (*Gesture of cutting off the air.*)

All that shows my bad luck! (*Tic.*) And yet, when I was twenty, life smiled on me! I had money, talent, no, not talent, but spirit. I smelled the flowers! And when I saw a woman pass by (Oh, any woman!), I felt (*Tic.*) glad to be alive.

Oh! Women!… That's why I took dancing classes; I worked enormously on my dancing.—But I never danced. I didn't dare, with my bad luck.

Oh! What I've seen in the way of charming young ladies! But I never spoke to them. And it's funny! They never spoke to me either.

I had too much bad luck! So, to forget my troubles, I indulged in debauchery. With money, you can have everything… Well! In my case, I got nothing for my money, or, if I got something, it was no fun. My friends broke the windows, and I always paid the fines.

They cost me a lot, all those fines! So I joined the Nitwit Club (it's the most serious) to make back by gambling what I lost in debauchery. (*Tic.*)

I'm quite the gambler—I have superstitions, charms. I say to myself: Unlucky in love, lucky at cards. You understand? Well, I reversed the proverb.—So I play, I lose. Anatole tells me: Keep going, your luck will change! I keep going, I lose. Anatole encourages me: I double, I triple, I quadruple my stakes and at last… I lost everything, or almost.

All I had left was my millstone quarry in La Ferté-sous-Jouarre!… I was in despair… Anatole said:—Poor guy! You can tell there's no hangman's rope in his pocket.

At those words, I return home. I liquidate my securities. I send Jean, my valet, to pay this terrifying debt, and I sit down to think things over. I often think things over, because of my bad luck. The hangman's rope… It's a superstition! A charm! It has to work, it will work for me.

I had two and a half francs left in my pocket. I leave the house like a mad dog. I walked, I ran! I see a shop: Martin, ropemaker. I enter.— Give me two and a half francs of hangman's rope.

Martin smiles; he jokes:—I don't carry it, but here's some fine merchandise to make some.

I take the packet of rope, I return home and have dinner. I say to Jean:—Tomorrow, at five past eleven, come wake me up, or I'll fire you!

That's how I talk to him, and he's devoted to me. (*Tic.*)

After dinner, I think things over, and… I go to bed. I slept! Like a rock.

Bad luck helps you sleep.

The next day, I wake up—it's ten o'clock. I start to think things over. My millstone quarry in La Ferté-sous-Jouarre, it makes money, it makes money… I don't know how much it makes… My notary knows. I don't think it's much. And besides, I can't live in a quarry. And what about food? You can't eat millstones.

There was the packet of rope on the footstool. Not a minute to lose:—Jean was due at five past eleven!

I get up on the footstool,—in the middle of the ceiling I unhook a Chinese lantern I use as a night light; I thread the rope through the ring, I get down from the footstool, and I think things over... I often think things over, because of my bad luck. (*Tic.*)

It was three past eleven. I make a slipknot, no, a sailor's knot. At school I was very good at making nets and sailor's knots. I look over my toilette and my past life.

It was four past eleven; I get back on the footstool.

I put the sailor's knot around my neck, and, with one eye on the clock, I think things over.

My heart was pounding as if I had fifty louis at stake on the green felt.

Four and a half minutes past eleven. I hear Jean's heavy steps coming to wake me up. Jean approaches, he's about to turn the doorknob...

Oof! I kick away the footstool, and...

Well! People generally have the wrong idea about hanging.

I felt like... like some kind of... well! I felt... no, really, I can't explain it. Really, to understand me, you yourself should... but you wouldn't want to.

At last, when I came to, I was on my bed, drenched in Melissa water.

I wanted to cry out: Where's the rope? But I couldn't because my throat was so sore. It's curious, that soreness! (*Tic.*)

This is what happened.

I was barely in the air when Jean came in, saw me dancing around and cut me down at once.

I wanted to get up to find the rope, but my back hurt. That's something doctors don't know about! What mysterious connection is there between the neck and the back!

I got a rubdown, and that evening I returned, limping badly, to the club. I had my rope in my pocket.

They were playing for high stakes. I bet my millstone quarry on a coup of baccarat and... I win!

I bet everything I had: money and quarry, and I still won.

At last, I passed five times. I had won back my whole fortune, except a meadow and ten cows out west. I thought it prudent to stop there. Besides, nobody would bet against me.

Well! Doesn't that seem lucky?

Not at all. Since that time, I've gambled until I'm blue in the face, and I can't win or lose a thing. My luck is neither good nor bad. That's not lucky!

I almost forgot to tell you how I became engaged—trusting in the power of my rope. Tomorrow I marry a very acceptable person whom I don't detest, certainly, whom I even respect. But that's not love, love that must be appeased!

When I told Anatole all this, he said a very remarkable thing:— You're not a real hanged man, you weren't hanged legally, in the name of the law, according to the court, for a real crime. Your rope only worked halfway.

What he said is true;—and he added that to get really lucky, I'd have to get married and be…

Well! You can see the strangeness of my fate! Given the respectable and peaceful nature of my fiancée, that will never happen. (*Tic.*)…

I'll go order the cars… Good night.

THE MAN WHO MADE A DISCOVERY

I live in Vaugirard. I have to get back there. I have just a minute to tell you about my discovery.

Vaugirard isn't very pretty, but it's quiet, and for brain work, you need quiet. My wife doesn't like Vaugirard (women don't understand brain work); besides, she goes out every day: she goes to Paris, to visit her old classmates, or to go shopping. So I stay home alone and do my brain work.

My wife has a cousin who's an artillery officer: that's what put me on the right path. He has dinner with us every day, and I explain my ideas to him. He's a good listener. He wears pants with three red stripes: two wide and one narrow, in the middle.

But where I really started to question things was at the railway station. I was waiting for my wife, who was coming back with her cousin. I stared at those four endless tracks, and my brain was working. I was bored; it's when you're bored that you discover things. I looked up, and counted the telegraph wires; there were twenty-two of them.

They arrived (my wife and her cousin) very late. I was very close to understanding the situation, but I still hadn't thought it over enough, or observed it enough.

Observe! Observe! That's how you discover things.

It was in the Botanical Garden that a light switched on, all of a sudden, in my head. My wife had sent me to the hospital, to take a half-dozen woolen stockings to her old nurse.

It was very hot, and as I leave the hospital, I see the Botanical Garden across the street. Greenery! Shade! (There's not much greenery or shade in Vaugirard.)

I enter the Botanical Garden, and I come to the zebra pen. He was crazy, that zebra; he was galloping around his little pen... really galloping!

Then I understood everything; my discovery was complete.

I say to myself: the zebra, famous for its speed, has stripes. Therefore, everything that has stripes is fast, and, reciprocally, everything that is fast has stripes. I'll prove it to you.

It was late, I take a streetcar; it goes fast: it's a kind of train, it has tracks, those are stripes.

On the streetcar I recapitulated: my wife's cousin... striped pants, he walks quickly. He commands a battery of striped cannons.

What goes faster than cannonballs?

I was on the upper deck: a few raindrops started falling. There was a storm... Lightning! That's something quick! It stripes the sky! It's striped, like the telegraph wires, those stripes in the countryside, where electricity travels so fast!... It was raining very hard, but rain falls quickly: it's striped, rain is, like the telegraph wires, but in the other direction.

The rain stops. On the boulevard Montparnasse I hear: "Here they are! All fresh! Here they are!" It was a woman selling fish. The fish did look fresh; they must have arrived quickly. Aha! They have striped backs.

Oh, I could keep listing the proofs of my discovery. But you aren't scientists; it would bore you.

But wait! One last example... The mail is always late in the winter; the post office blames the snow blocking the roads. Well! That's not it at all! In winter the mailmen wear pants that are a solid color, but in summer they wear striped twill! So the mail arrives sooner.

Do you like that? Another example, then: this will be the last one. My wife's cousin plays piano; he plays notes; he plays masses of them every second!

Very well! Where does he find the notes? On striped paper. The piano itself is striped (the strings)!

You're not scientists. You'll say to me: this is all just theory. What good is it?

But the applications are immense! You can ensure the speed of all correspondence, thanks to a thoroughly striped costume, in all seasons, for all employees.

On the other hand, that kind of uniform should be absolutely forbidden to cashiers... In fact, it's infinite, it's superb!

Well! You know how people are! I ran back home, I was in a sweat; the rain had soaked my hat, and made black stripes on my face.

My wife hadn't gone out yet. Her cousin was also there. He seemed to be hot.—I cried out as I entered, "I found out everything! I understand everything now!"

My wife fainted; my cousin grabbed his sword and tried to leave. (They don't understand science!)

I poured a pitcher of water over my wife's head, and when she felt better, I explained my discovery: everything with stripes goes fast.

Believe it or not, but she burst out laughing, laughing her head off! I thought she would faint again. And her cousin laughed too! It was just a nervous response: they don't understand science.

It doesn't matter, they'll still profit from it: I bought my wife a striped dress so she'll be back for dinner sooner.

I have to go; I'll be late. See? (*He indicates his pants.*) No stripes!

(POSSIBLE ENDING GAG. (*He returns.*) I just realized: they say "the dead go fast." It's quite simple:—They're barred... from life.)

THE VIOLIN

I'll tell you all about my life:
I am a very happy man.
I spent ten years in music school,
And won two prizes out of three.
And yet my pockets were unfilled,
My shoes were gaping at the heels,
I dined on thirty-second notes!
I counted on my violin.

My classmates, sorry fellows all,
Who scraped the catgut on the wood,
Got by, like me, on idle dreams.
For what's a hundred francs a month?
(And out in those suburban shows,
That's all we got.) It took so long
To walk out there. More than a mile,
While carrying your violin.

Though I'm an artist, I'm no fool;
And from then on, I told myself
That working my chromatic scale,
I'd starve there in my humble flat.
"Let's try to find another way
To earn enough to buy some broth.
When I can order cuts of beef,
Then I'll unpack my violin."

I had a strong and sturdy chest:
I locked my instrument within,
And tossed the key into the Seine…
If not for that, I'd still have scraped.

My friends, still famished and in debt,
Called me a traitor, a bourgeois.
But more than one has died of want,
Once he had sold his violin.

I grabbed the bull by both his horns:
And made myself a grocer's boy.
O violin of boundless charms,
I earned more than by sawing you!
I ate my soup, bowl after bowl,
My beefsteak and my loaf of bread.
That puts more fat upon your leg
Than playing on the violin.

Oh, it was hard at first. The pay
Was meager; there were many times
I grumbled at my sorry lot.
I always seemed to hit my hands;
My hands, which used to have such grace,
And hold the bow with such aplomb.
I soaked them in molasses then!
I often missed my violin.

Ah! When I started, it was rough!
One day my boss surprised me in
A strange and awkward attitude.
(In Paris, art pursues you so!)
Distracted by a passing song,
Like some grotesque Apollo, I
Was fingering a salted cod
As if it were a violin!

But I adjusted to the job;
With honesty and proper zeal,
You're bound to gain success at last.
I even stashed a bit away.

The boss, to meet a pressing bill,
Required a little wherewithal.
I loaned him an amount ten times
The value of my violin.

The boss's daughter, by the way,
Had quite a knack for keeping books,
But she was very nice as well.
And I was tempted, being young.
For my success in wooing her,
My loan had been a decent start.
I'm sure I would have pleased her more
If I had had my violin!

By now I'm sure you've guessed the rest:
(Does business do away with love?)
And soon the two of us were one.
The boss remarked to me one day:
Now that my fortune has been made,
I'll move away, to far Ablon.
So take my daughter and my shop,
They're worth more than your violin.

And then the wedding bells, and then
The honeymoon; ten years went by.
I'm happy now! My fortune's made,
I have three lovely kids as well.
And yet the oldest worries me:
(The eaglet has his father's wings!)
I found him at a neighbor's house
This evening, with a violin.

I seized his ear, and pulled him home.
(He played quite well, the little scamp!)
Now I'm the one who's waking up,
Henceforth my life belongs to art.

So I shall let you hear tonight
My specialty, my concert piece.
It's by Rossini, brisk and sweet.
My dream! My cherished violin!

(*He opens the case.*)

For twenty years, you've slumbered here,
Mute, at the bottom of your case.
Like wines that ripen in the cask,
You're only mellower today!
Come sing the old sonorous song
Of valleys and of mountain peaks!
We still have happy days ahead,
My violin! My violin!

(*He picks up the violin and tries to tune it.*)

So, la, re, mi. (*A string breaks.*) The highest string
Just broke, but that's of no concern.
It's very old!… It fell apart!…
Three strings will be enough for me.
Re, la, re, so. Is this in tune?
The G string makes a buzzing sound.
A G should have a stronger tone.
It's caught a cold, my violin.

Yes! I recall. The overture
Begins with passagework in E;
No, wait, in F. What torture! Oh!
It seems to me it slept too long.
Let's start out with a simple scale,
And go up slowly note by note.
It's out of tune! It's vile, it's sour!
Now I can't play the violin!

(*He throws the instrument into the case.*)

For these last twenty years, I've soaked
My hands in fish and tartar sauce,
Detergent, kerosene and oil!
That doesn't keep the fingers fit.
And yet, I still love music so!
Who'll play cotillions for you, then?
Of course, my son! (Artistic soul!)
I'll give to him my violin.

Poor child! And I who punished him
For having talent, just tonight!
And yet, before I'm dead and gone,
How else should I spend my estate?
Why not? He won't need common sense;
He'll work as hard as he desires.
I hope that he'll devote himself
Completely to the violin.

PROPERTY

Monologue performed by Coquelin Cadet.

(On entering, he gives his hat and cane to a servant.)

Here, Baptiste, take my hat, my cane, my coat... (*Alarmed.*) Say! I left my coat over there! Baptiste, go get it, from M. Dubois, 333, rue Ménilmontant, 333, the three hunchbacks, as they say in lotto. Because I need it, my coat; it keeps me warm, my coat! (*Cry.*) Oh la la! What am I saying, my hat, my cane, my coat; I'm becoming a proprietor! I caught their disease! If I ever set foot in that house again!... I'd want to lose MY name, no, not MY, *the... the...* name! I'd put MY hand in the fire—no THE hand in the fire.—It's just that, you see, when you've heard that for eight months, three times a week—the good man (God preserve me from ever seeing him again!) and his wife, and his maid (all cut from the same cloth), you'd understand—I mean you wouldn't understand—that I made it out alive.

—It does you good not to be at home! Not to say to yourself: "I'm in my own home!"

—I rented a little pied-à-terre in Le Raincy; I need to finish my thesis for my degree. The law, it's useless, but you have to go through with it anyway.—I didn't tell anyone my address, it's not because of the law, it's because of Ménilmontant, number 333; I know I seem crazy, sick even. But really, I'll explain it for you.—My godfather who never leaves Livarot had, forty years ago, a friend, a M. Dubois he knew in Paris; he recommended me to this M. Dubois, and when I came, to study law (and what good is it!) in Paris, I went to see him, this FRIEND. M. Dubois, who was, so to speak, my guardian, (he had a kind of authority over me) is a former debt collector. He still collects from time to time—as an amateur.—He forced me to have dinner with him three times a week. That seems very nice of him; me, I must seem like an ingrate, a scoundrel,—well, you'll see—his wife—she's still not bad, a bit plump—it must seem very agreeable to have dinner three times a week with those people.—Jeannette, the maid, who took care of me!... She's nice too, that maid—it must seem charming, absolutely charming! Well, it's not! You'll see, I'll tell you how it went whenever I went there. I entered: hello, Monsieur Dubois, hello, Madame Dubois. Hello, Jeannette. M. Dubois asks me: "What's the news this evening? Ah no, I'll read it to you, MY news.—Jeannette, MY paper." Jeannette brings the paper, he says: "And MY tape? You know quite well, I like to cut MY tape myself. MY wife, ah, pardon, Madame Dubois has her own paper, and I don't think, I'm sure she would never permit herself to cut MY tape. Very well, go!"

Jeannette leaves, nudging me in the back with her elbow.—And then at the table, Madame Dubois isn't there yet:

—Jeannette, go tell Madame that when I have MY almost god-son at MY table, she could very well not keep us waiting. The soup is served. M. Dubois:—What is MY soup this evening?—Potatoes and leeks, whispers M. Dubois.—MY dear Paul (that's me), taste MY wine.—What do you think of MY dining room? MY chairs are nice, aren't they? They're cane. I have MY canework done by MY craftsman.

Then Jeannette brings some kind of mediocre slop. M. Dubois goes on (you'll see if you could stand it), he goes on:—MY ragout is made in MY kitchen, from a recipe handed down in MY family.—You're not drinking?—I do believe I'm not drinking.—I feel dazed. I look at him like this. (*Face.*) And then, Madame Dubois looks at me like this. (*Face.*) (I believe it's called a come-hither look.) She's still not bad, Madame Dubois. Her stew? He asks me if it's good, I say yes; I feel dazed. We eat a lot of things. M. Dubois goes on—he says: MY salad, MY oil and after that, MY pears, MY coffee, MY Chartreuse.

And he pours himself quite a dose!… while saying that he's cold. And he still goes on, to Jeannette, MY slippers, with your permission, MY dear Paul, because after all you're MY guest, I'm almost your god-father. You're MY own Paul, after all.

Please explain to me why things like that send chills down your spine. It seems like nothing, but when it continues three times a week, eight months of the year! Well, I'll give you some idea of it, by telling you what happened last night.—I arrived at their building at a quarter to seven (dinner was at seven). I went to ring the bell, Jeannette was on the doorstep. I heard M. Dubois crying in the apartment: "Coralie, what were you doing with MY tobacco? What can I put in MY snuffbox this evening? You know very well that if I don't have MY pinch (*Gesture.*) it ruins MY dinner.—I must go immediately to the shop across from the Théâtre-Français (a dismal neighborhood) to restock MY supply. I haven't had dinner yet. Too bad, I'll eat in a restaurant. Jeannette! MY hat and MY umbrella. I'm leaving. Good evening, Paul: eat MY soup and MY beef in peace, visit with MY wife, pardon, Madame Dubois; serious matters oblige me to leave now. I enter, I see a pot of tobacco—tobacco for the nose—overturned, and all the tobacco on the floor; Jeannette, sweeping it up, was sneezing and laughing. Madame Dubois wasn't sneezing, but she was laughing a little, anyway.

Madame Dubois—it was one of the few times I heard her speak.— (*Simpering and impatient voice.*)

—Jeannette, quick, quick, bring dinner.

—The peas aren't cooked.

—It doesn't matter, it doesn't matter. We'll eat them tomorrow. She had a funny look on her face, Madame Dubois. "Jeannette, set the table, MY little table, in MY little yellow living room. It's cold in the dining room, and there are just two of us." (*Coy look.*)

—What I ate, my word, I have no idea. It was half burned, half raw, there was nothing to drink. And then Madame Dubois told me interminable stories, stories about bandits;—and from time to time she said: "I'd like to be your mother."

My mother, my mother, what for? She's no longer young, but she's still too young to be my mother. And then too, she talked about the Ideal!... the Ideal!... things about the philosophy of the heart... renewal... the springtime of life!... Well, I don't remember, I didn't understand any of it. And then suddenly, she started rattling off a bunch of things: MY head, MY hand, MY arms, MY hair, MY family, MY reputation! The poor woman had caught her husband's disease. Me, my, mine.—Fortunately, Jeannette enters like a bullet. Madame Dubois, who was sprawled on the sofa, cries out. She gets up.

(*Voice.*)

—Who called you, Jeannette?

(*Another voice.*)

—Madame, I've come to ask for your orders, for MY shopping tomorrow. I finished cleaning MY kitchen, MY dishes are done, MY knives are sharpened, MY oven is turned off, MY sink is washed! Would Madame like to tell me what to get in MY shopping?

Madame Dubois thinks, thinks, thinks, and comes up with nothing. (*Voice.*) "Say something, Paul! Me, I don't know anymore, I don't know anymore."

Me, I say:—Jeannette, you'll make some soup, a plate of meat, a plate of vegetables, and a dessert,—you know, like in the restaurant on the little card.—That's it! That's it! said Madame Dubois. She was clapping her hands. (*Gesture.*) Jeannette, you can go visit your aunt this evening. Go! But Jeannette put her finger on her chin (it's not bad, that chin, and her finger too, in spite of washing dishes). (*Voice.*) "Monsieur Paul said soup. But what kind of soup?" Madame Dubois was annoyed and said: "I don't care! Paul, tell her what soup you like."

—It doesn't matter, I'm not having dinner here tomorrow.

—Tell her what soup you like anyway, M. Dubois will eat it.

It was getting boring, all this talk about the soup! I say at random: "Make my soup sorrel!"

Then Jeannette: "Ah! That depends, Monsieur Paul, (she was swinging back and forth on her broom, and seemed to be mocking me). There's sorrel soup, and there's sorrel soup.—So, me, this is how I make it: I peel MY sorrel and MY chervil. I wash MY sorrel, but never MY chervil. I take MY butter (a lump as big as an apricot) with MY wooden spoon. I melt it in MY saucepan, I add MY sorrel; not MY chervil yet. It heats up, and I stir it, and keep stirring, and turning up MY fire." (*Gesture of blowing with the breath.*) Then Madame Dubois became furious and said:

—What does Monsieur Paul care, about your sorrel soup! Go back to your kitchen.

—I'm finished, Madame… I slice MY bread very thin into MY tureen, I break MY egg on MY bread, I dilute MY yolk with a little water. Then I chop up MY chervil; I put it, splash! into MY sorrel broth, and I let it soak!…

(*Gesture.*)

Madame Dubois was purple with rage. She leapt up to strangle Jeannette. But Jeannette ran away. Oh la la! Madame Dubois fell back on the sofa. "That maid is killing me!" She was killing me too! Every-

one was killing me, especially Madame Dubois: "MY heart, MY reputation, etc., etc." And Jeannette: "MY towel, MY dishes." Enough! I
was dying. I said: "Madame, I'm not feeling well… all of a sudden…
I must go…"

—Stay, Paul! I have some orange-flower water.

—No, no, no! I need fresh air! Air, air, air!… And I galloped off like
a zebra. It was there that I left my overcoat, in the anteroom, it bothers
me because of two letters with patchouli in my pocket.

On the mezzanine, I meet M. Dubois coming back with a yellow
package under his arm. "You're leaving already! I have MY Macouba
tobacco, from the end of November, and MY bean! I have the real bean
(not the fake one they put in the Epiphany cake, no!). The Tonka bean,
from the guaiac tree. Come back upstairs, we'll have a little chat." A
chat? Horrors! Horrors! "MY heart, MY dishes, MY boots!" Oh no,
I've had enough! Oh no, I'll never set foot in that place again. And I'll
stay well hidden in Le Raincy. I'll finish my law thesis (what good is it!)
because I have to! Yes, in Le Raincy, in the greenery, in peace, not at
MY place, not at SOMEONE ELSE'S place, but at an inn. (*He listens.*)
Well, here's Baptiste with my coat. I'm leaving! Dubois might find me.
Good night.

THE SAD MONOLOGUE

(Coquelin Cadet, from *The Art of Speaking the Monologue*.)

"The Salt Herring" is less a monologue than a severe ditty, whose emotion is rather hard to explain: these imperfect and rhythmic scraps of verse, which fall like raindrops, will not always captivate the crowd; but when they do provoke laughter, their effect is considerable.

I give "The Salt Herring" as an example of a completely different monologue, based on nothing, and succeeding due to its remarkable stupidity. This story was written to lull a child to sleep. We guarantee the success of "The Salt Herring" before artists and in seaports. I cannot recommend it for all audiences.

THE SALT HERRING

There was a great white wall—bare, bare, bare,
[Cry "The Salt Herring" in a loud voice. Don't move your body, be absolutely immobile. The audience must get the feeling of a black line against a white background.

This is an effect I will call pictorial, but necessary to the harmony of the scene you are about to create. Attack with a solid voice: "The Salt Herring." Say "There was a great white wall—bare, bare, bare," so that one feels the wall, straight and rigid, and because it would be boring to be that monotonous, break the monotony: draw out the sound on the third "bare," that will enlarge the wall, and almost show its dimensions to your listeners.]

Against the wall, a ladder—high, high, high,
[Same intention and same intonation as for the first line, and to give the idea of a very high ladder, deliver the last "high" in falsetto (an absolutely unexpected note), it will get a laugh, and will be in keeping with the fantasy of the text.]

And on the ground, a salt herring—dry, dry, dry.
[Point to the ground, and say "salt herring" with a blank expression that calls attention to the unfortunate herring, your voice will naturally

be very dry for the three adjectives "dry, dry, dry."]

He comes, holding in his hands—dirty, dirty, dirty,

[Sustain the voice, and let the rhythm be heard in the other stanzas as in the first. "He" is the character, we don't know who "he" is. Let him be seen, show him, this "he" who moves you, you the actor, and depict the disgust one feels for a man who never washes his hands, on the words "dirty, dirty, dirty."]

A heavy hammer, a big nail—sharp, sharp, sharp,

[Lower one shoulder, as though carrying a hammer too heavy for you, and show the nail, pointing your index finger at the audience, and emphasize "sharp, sharp, sharp," so that the nail is driven firmly into their attention.]

A ball of string—big, big, big.

[Spread your hands, away from your sides by degrees, with each "big, big, big." "He" is loaded down, a heavy hammer, a big pointed nail, and an enormous ball of string. That's not nothing, you must show the burden under which "he" is bent.]

Then he climbs the ladder—high, high, high,

[Same business for the "high, high, high," as before, the falsetto note at the end, the repetition may get a laugh.]

And hammers in the sharp nail—toc, toc, toc,

[The actions of a man driving a nail with a hammer, make the "toc, toc, toc," ring out forcefully, without changing the sound.]

High on the great white wall—bare, bare, bare.

[Keep your tone of voice very firm, draw out the last "bare" again, and make a flat gesture with your hand to show the regularity of the wall.]

He drops the hammer—which falls, which falls, which falls,

[Lower the pitch by degrees to give the idea of a falling hammer. Look at the audience on the first "which falls," again on the second, then glance at the ground before the third, and then a third look at the audience when you say the third "which falls," and wait for the effect that must produce.]

Ties to the nail the string—long, long, long,

[Draw out the sound gradually on "long," and let the last "long" be immensely long, a break in your voice in the middle of the last letter will give a comic flavor to the word.]

And, at the end, the salt herring—dry, dry, dry.

[Stress the third "dry" with a more and more pitiful expression.]

He descends the ladder—high, high, high,

[Same business as before when he was climbing, only the inflection of each "high" grows softer, the first in falsetto, the second medium, and the third in a deep voice. Musical.]

Carries it off with the hammer—heavy, heavy, heavy,

[Bend under the hammer as you go. You're broken, you can't go on, the hammer is too heavy, don't forget.]

And then he goes away—far, far, far.

[Increase each "far," on the third you can put your hand over your eyes to shield them, to see "him" at a considerable distance, and after you see him far, far away, say the last "far."]

And since then, the salt herring—dry, dry, dry,

[More and more pitiful.]

At the end of that string—long, long, long,

[Draw out the voice in a very melancholy tone on each "long," always with the break; don't worry, it's a running gag.]

Has been swinging very slowly—forever, forever, forever.

[Very sad. And a swinging gesture on "forever, forever, forever." Finish by lowering your voice on the third "forever," for the story is over. The last lines are just a reassuring postscript for the listener.]

I wrote this story—simple, simple, simple,

[Emphasize "simple," to make the audience say, "Oh yes! *Simple!*"]

To annoy adults—serious, serious, serious,

[Very stern; let them feel the official high white starched collars that don't like this kind of foolishness. Open your mouth wide on the last "serious," like a Monsieur Prudhomme who is very offended.]

And to amuse children—little, little, little.

[Very sweetly, with a smile, gradually lower your hand with each "little" to indicate the heights and ages of the children. Bow and make a quick exit.]

· ·

This is how to recite "The Salt Herring" in its entirety. As you can see, I let nothing escape me in this work, which has great comic power if the audience is not made of wood. For true devotees of laughter, I will add that "The Salt Herring," translated into Italian, was recited on the stage of La Scala in Milan, and was forbidden by the censor. It was thought to contain certain political allusions.

I would never recommend "The Salt Herring" as an opening piece for bourgeois families, it is important that the performer try to assess the intellectual state of the rooms in which he monologues, to calibrate the imaginative understanding of the guests; if the stories prepared in the studio fit the taste of people who have dined copiously while chatting about current events, if they will not be too surprised, on rising from the table, by such preposterous recitations.

It is essential to create an atmosphere, to soften too brusque a transition between reality and fantasy, to begin with works that can be listened to with no effort whatsoever. "The Bilboquet," a true masterpiece by Charles Cros, would be entirely unwelcome at the start of a program; you must know how to measure out your repertory, and develop a crescendo.

The fierce imagination of Morand or Sivry would only frighten the guests at the beginning of an evening; Paul Bilhaud and Georges Moynet, frank and human monologists, are more suited to open an informal program. Afterwards, unleash the fullblooded wild ones, those that take us on such beautiful voyages far from reality!

You must, I repeat, know what you *must say*. Before a judge, before doctors, before artists, in the middle of the suburb of Saint-Germain or twenty miles from Paris, different things are required; for that you must stock your memory with many monologues, and have a good selection at your disposal to answer the needs of different audiences. This kind of recitation is so special! A monologue that delights one house will fall flat in another. Therefore, study your audiences carefully, and try to get inside, if not their souls, at least their spleens. Try to guess what will make them laugh most easily and most agreeably. I cannot say more about this subtle question; I leave to the devotees of monologues the task of familiarizing themselves with the difficult art of the nuances involved in pleasing and charming audiences who appreciate humorous pieces.

OBSESSION

(Coquelin Cadet, from *The Art of Speaking the Monologue*.)

[You must begin with a lamentable expression on your face, recalling those of people suffering from seasickness, aboard a ship.]

Ah! I'm very sick.
[Let intense illness be felt.]

The other evening, two days ago, I went to the theater, to the Délassements.
[Put great fatigue into the word "Délassements."]

A delightful play, a charming little air, how did it go? Wait, tra, la, la.
[The tune "Saltarello," by Hervé. Sing it loudly and long.]

I sang it merrily, me, as I returned home, letting the heels of my boots ring out on the sidewalk. Tra, la, la, la.
[Put your two thumbs in the opening of your waistcoat—an expansive expression, the attitude of a man digging his heels into the sidewalk, sing loudly and merrily.]

I live far away. I ring, ding! ding! ding! ding!
[On the same tune as "tra, la, la," the actions of a man ringing vigorously, while singing in a high voice "ding! ding!" to give the impression of a doorbell rung to awaken a stupid and sleepy doorman.]

My concierge takes an hour to let me in, I was dying of cold, tra, la, la.
[Pull up the collar of your suit and shiver, "tra, la, la," from deep within the collar of your suit, you are not warm.]

Finally! He opens! I run upstairs, four steps at a time, tra, la, la.

[Gleefully. It's fun to sing on the stairs.]

I enter my room, I undress, tra, la, la.
[While imitating a man removing his coat, his waistcoat, his pants, everything, continue the "tra, la, la" in an undertone until the audience laughs.]

I go to bed and lose no time in falling deliciously asleep, tra, la, la.
[Close your eyes with an extraordinarily beatific smile; hum "tra, la, la," punctuating it with sonorous snores. You sleep deliciously while singing.]

The next morning, a sunbeam shines up my nose. I wake up, tra, la, la.
[Very high on the "tra, la, la." It is the tyrannical and victorious air that retakes possession of its victim and picks up again in the morning with renewed energy. Tra, la, la! (shrill).]

I jump out of bed, tra, la, la. I duck my head in cold water, tra, la, la.
[Gurgling the "tra, la, la," so that one hears the splashing of a man plunging into his wash basin, and dripping water from his mouth, eyes, and nose.]

I dry off with a towel! Tra, la, la!
[With your right hand, seem to dry yourself with a fluffy towel, energetically, the obsession starting to get on your nerves, and you avenge yourself on your face.]

A knock at the door: I go to open it, tra, la, la.
[Slave of the song.]

It's my concierge. Ah! You certainly made me wait, you, last night, tra, la, la.
["Last night" and "tra, la, la" running together, furiously.]

A letter, let's see, tra, la, la.

[Very expressive mimicry, he reads with his eyes, then repeats a "tra, la, la," he continues his reading with his eys and interrupts it with a "tra, la, la," finally he emits a heart-rending and comical "Ah!"]

Ah! My poor aunt!
[He keeps his eyes fixed on the letter a few seconds, stricken with grief, then bursts into a huge "tra, la, la" that clearly expresses the desperate state of the soul!]

Not a minute to lose. I pull on my coat, I forget my umbrella. I was devastated, tra, la, la.
[Very high on the "tra, la, la.]

I tumble downstairs, four steps at a time. First cab I see, I jump in: "To the Western Station." Oh, my poor aunt! What a terrible misfortune! It's awful! Tra, la, la.
["Awful" and "tra, la, la" running together. One should have the impression of a tune absolutely affixed to the unhappy man, who can no longer shake it off, the more he sings it now, the more it fills him, alas!]

A half hour later, I arrive in Versailles to receive my aunt's final breath, tra, la, la!
[Your face literally convulsed with sorrow, a rubber-faced grimace, dry your tears while singing "tra, la, la" lugubriously.]

I have to run here and there for the funeral arrangements, and always that air! Tra, la, la.
[Impressively.]

And even following her to her final resting place, tra, la, la.
[With the bowed head of an heir following a funeral procession, your hand in your waistcoat, your face completely contrite, your lip brooding, sing "tra, la, la" as if there were crepe on it, mezza-voce, very softly, but implacable, a "tra, la, la" of deep mourning.]
A man says to me: "You seem quite devastated." Ah, monsieur, let's

not talk about it! It! It!

["It! It! It!" To the tune of "tra, la, la," very loud.]

It's a great loss for you!—"I am inconsolable!" Tra, la, la.
[Louder and louder.]

Oh! That air! Well, since it won't leave me alone, I'll use it to express my sorrow.

[Singing with your whole soul:]

I have just lost my dear old auntie,
And she is never coming back.
Maybe the will she left was scanty,
But I can buy a suit of black.

So she can move around at leisure,
She has a box with lots of room.
Nobody has a bit of pleasure
When you can't move around your tomb!

[Let the audience think that it's over; that the unhappy obsessive has spit out the venom that poisoned his existence.]

I return to Paris, and always that air! Tra, la, la!
{He sings it again in a frenzy, the disease worsens.]

At the station I knock everyone over! Tra, la, la.
[Let it be felt that he flees, pursued by the song-specter, and that he knocks over the nannies, old people, and dogs found in Montparnasse Station.]

I take a street, tra, la, la. Another, tra, la, la.
[Singing with frightening insistence; the tune is embedded in his brain from now on, and his tongue works in spite of himself, moved by a superior power.]

What? So, I'm going to sing all my life? Tra, la, la.
[Making a frightful grimace, of unparalleled bitterness.]

No, I would rather die! I reach the Seine, I jump in, I drown; glub! glub! glub!

[Let him be felt at the bottom of the Seine, swimming and singing "Saltarello" fifteen feet underwater, the "glub, glub" very sad: this is no bottle gurgling!]

I wake up in the rescue station for the drowned and asphyxiated, tra, la, la, la.

[Very loud, the tune seems to have been cleansed by the water; you must sing it in a very clear voice.]

I look at my clothes.
[Quite devastated.]

I spat out the water, tra, la, la.

[Opening your mouth and releasing a hiccup, like a man who has vomited enough water to fill several buckets.]

But I kept the air!!! And I'll always have it! Tra, la, la.

[Exit, singing in a desperate way, the audience must feel that you are stuck with it for life, that air.]

THE DEATH OF CHARLES CROS

(Alphonse Allais, 1888)

Our poor friend Charles Cros is dead.

I knew him well and liked him very much, and although I knew he had been ill and weak for a long time, I was sadly shocked by his sudden death.

It will remain one of the great pains of my life that I was not warned early enough to shake his hand one last time.

Poor Cros! I can still see him on the day I first met him. It was, if I'm not mistaken, in '76. How time flies!

That morning, I had read in the *Rappel* a scientific article by Victor Meunier, which seemed like a fairy tale.

A young man had just invented a bizarre instrument that recorded the human voice, and even all other sounds, and which not only transcribed the vibrations, but reproduced those noises as many times as one wished.

The instrument was called the *paléographe*. The theory behind it was of patriarchal simplicity.

The next day, thanks to my friend Lorin, I met Charles Cros, the inventor of the marvelous apparatus that Mr. Edison was to patent a year later.

Charles Cros struck me at once as I always knew him, a being miraculously gifted in every way, a strangely personal and charming poet, a true scientist, a disconcerting fantasist, and, what's more, a sure and true friend.

What did he lack to become a successful man, honored and decorated? Almost nothing, a bit of that cowardly and servile bourgeoisism his noble artistic nature always refused.

He wrote superb verses that earned him nothing, wrote as a lark those monologues that made Coquelin Cadet famous, had brilliant scientific ideas, invented the phonograph, color photography, the photophone (in his *Cerebral Mechanics*, Charles Cros described a theoretical device that caused hearty laughter in the Academy of Sciences: light that speaks! Two years later, an Englishman invented the same apparatus, which he called the "photophone," and was awarded a prize of 100,000 francs by the same Academy).

All of us, his friends at the *Chat Noir*, who loved poor Cros so much, send our sorrowful greetings to his family.

ALPHONSE ALLAIS

A weepy, boring, and sponging poet has indulged, concerning Cros's funeral, in some scandalous personal publicity. The individual in question, whom, for his lachrymatory and gelatinously sympathetic ditties, Salis had welcomed onto the staff of the *Chat Noir*, is seriously invited, for the sake of his derriere, to no longer appear.

A. A.

CHARLES CROS AND MR. EDISON

(Alphonse Allais, 1889)

I found myself, last week, aboard the *François Premier*, a ship that runs between Honfleur and Le Havre. Not far from me, a gentleman, an officer of the Legion of Honor, perorated and gesticulated to a group of well-dressed men and elegant women.

An occasional shout, from time to time, indicated an outburst of enthusiasm.

"That man," he proclaimed, "the government should welcome as a Messiah!"

They should have erected Arches of Trumph for him.

And whereas the Shah of Persia was greeted with unprecedented celebrations, they receive this man, him, like a common citizen. It's a disgrace for France!

The officer of the Legion of Honor was referring to Edison.

I went up to him, and, when the gentleman had consented to stop talking, I asked him politely:

"Excuse me, monsieur, but what has he done that's so extraordinary, this Edison?"

"What! What has he done that's extraordinary! Why, a thousand inventions, each more glorious than the last!"

"Among others?"

"The phonograph, which is one of the most marvelous instruments of the age."

"The phonograph is indeed a marvelous instrument, and it's very unfortunate for Edison that he didn't invent it."

"Then who invented it?"

"Charles Cros, a great French scientist, a great poet, who died a year ago. He was the sole inventor of the phonograph, and I know what I'm talking about: *I was there*... And besides, what else has he invented, your Edison?"

"The telephone."

"Oh, no! That was Graham Bell... What else?"

"Electric lighting."

"No more than the telephone. Edison invented a system of in-candescent bulbs neither better, nor worse, than many others… What else?"

"So, Edison is an imbecile, in your opinion?"

"Far from it, but in my opinion, and in the opinion of many peo-ple better informed than you or me, Edison is an admirable *forger*, very skillful, very ingenious, always on the look-out for new ideas, putting a whole hive of engineers to work, and cleverly using each man's efforts. In that profession, you can earn many millions, but you don't deserve an Arch of Triumph. Besides, the legend of Edison, drawing every day a new invention from his steaming brain, has had its day in America, and the puff pieces that have filled the Paris papers for the last month couldn't make it into the smallest rag in New York, except for so many dollars a line."

We had arrived in Le Havre. The officer of the Legion of Honor left me, thoroughly vexed.

After that, I conceived the idea of restoring, as well as I could, to the memory of poor Charles Cros, some of the fame Edison had stolen from him. Besides, the task is simple: one need only cite the facts and dates.

In 1876, when I met Cros, he already had the idea of recording the vibrations of a sound by means of *tracks*, and of reproducing the sound by means of those tracks.

On April 30, 1877, he submitted to the Academy of Sciences a sealed letter, which was read, at his request, at the meeting on Decem-ber 3, 1877, and can be found in the *Records of the Academy of Sciences* (published by Gauthier-Villars).

In this note, Cros proposes to record, by means of a stylus, the vibrations of a membrane onto a flat surface blackened with soot, and forming a spiral (or onto a cylinder, forming a helix). The tracks are photographed, and made into an intaglio engraving. The point of the stylus, connected to the membrane, plunges into this undulating fur-row, which is made to rotate at an appropriate speed, and reproduces the original vibrations.

Several scientific columnists took an interest in the new apparatus, among others M. Victor Meunier, in several issues of *Le Rappel*, whose dates I don't have before me, and Father Leblanc, who wrote, in the

Semaine du Clergé (on October 10, 1877), a detailed article, describing, under the name of "phonograph," an apparatus identical to Edison's current instrument, except that the vibrations are not recorded on tinfoil.

Now, it was not until December 19, 1877, in a patent filed in Paris, that Edison proposed several methods for recording the vibrations of a sound. This patent, which is very long and very confused, is above all concerned with "recording electric phenomena by sound" (techniques having nothing to do with the phonograph, which is a purely mechanical intrument).

On January 15, 1878, Edison filed a certificate of addition to his patent, describing his phonograph as it now exists. In this patent, Edison proposes, as preferable to recording on a cylinder, using a flat spiral, a process suggested by Cros in his sealed letter of April 30.

Edison was then behind Charles Cros by eight and a half months.

Did he know about our friend's work, or was it just coincidence? It is a question that would be quite simple to elucidate, but which is none of our business.

Poor Cros had had other disappointments, and was to have many more after that.

We will only cite the "photophone," which he described in detail in his *Treatise on Cerebral Mechanics*, two years before that invention earned its "inventor" (?) a prize of a hundred thousand francs from the Academy of Sciences.

So, to summarize, the government of France was right not to erect Arches of Triumph to the famous Yankee handyman, but it would honor itself if it chose to remember that a brilliant French scientist, a great poet, Charles Cros, died poor, leaving a widow and two children.

ALPHONSE ALLAIS.

P. S.—Absent from Paris for some time, I am unaware if some paper has claimed, for our compatriot, the glory of the phonograph.

If some colleague, more suitable than I, wanted to do it, it would be to his credit. I need not add that I guarantee absolutely the correctness of the dates and facts cited above.

A. A.

NOTES

"Rhythmic Story for Little Children" (*Conte rhythmé pour les petits enfants*): *La Renaissance littéraire et artistique*, May 25, 1872.

This is the first draft of "The Salt Herring"; note that it's already outfitted with stage directions.

"The Salt Herring" (*Le Hareng saur*): *Le Coffret de Santal*, 1873; *Saynètes et Monologues*, third series (1878). In the 1879 edition of *Le Coffret de Santal*, Cros added the dedication to his son Guy, born February 2, 1879.

In *Le Tout-Paris*, August 30, 1880, Paul Allais noted that his brother Alphonse had recited "The Salt Herring" in English, at a meeting of the Hydropathes. George Eliot, in his book *Memoirs of My Dead Life*, gave an English version assumed to be Allais's. However, the book mentions neither Cros nor Allais, instead crediting it to the composer Ernest Cabaner, who had indeed set it to music. Here's the text from the 1906 edition of Moore's book:

THE SONG OF THE "SALT HERRING"

He came along holding in his hands dirty, dirty, dirty,
A big nail pointed, pointed, pointed,
And a hammer heavy, heavy, heavy,
He propped the ladder high, high, high,
Against the wall white, white, white,
He went up the ladder high, high,
Placed the nail pointed, pointed, pointed,
Against the wall—toc! toc! toc!
He tied to the nail a string long, long, long,
And at the end of it a salt herring dry, dry, dry,
Then letting fall the hammer heavy, heavy, heavy,
He got down from the ladder high, high, high,
Picked up the ladder and went away, away, away.

Since then at the end of the string long, long, long,
A salt herring dry, dry, dry,
Has swung slowly, slowly, slowly.
Now I have composed this story simple, simple, simple,
To make all serious men mad, mad, mad,
And to amuse little children tiny, tiny, tiny.

It differs from Cros's text in a number of ways, particularly in omitting the first three lines. Moore gave different versions in the 1923 and 1926 editions; it was the last of these that Edward Gorey illustrated in 1971, crediting the translation to Allais. I think it more likely that Moore was responsible.

Joris-Karl Huysmans wrote a prose poem called *Le Hareng saur* in 1874. Given the popularity of Cros's monologue, it may have been a response. Huysmans later dismissed Cros in his 1884 novel *À Rebours*, calling Cros's story "The Love Service" a "dismal failure." Huysmans's approach to the herring is certainly different from Cros's:

Your dress, O herring, is the palette of setting suns, the patina of old copper, the tarnished gold tints of Cordoba leather, the saffron and sandalwood shades of autumn leaves!

Your head, O herring, blazes like a golden helmet, and one might call your eyes black nails driven into copper circles.

All the sad and dreary nuances, all the bright and shining nuances deaden and enliven in turn your dress of scales.

Beside the bitumen, earth of Judea and Cassel, Scheele's green and burnt umber, Van Dyck's brown, Florentine bronze, and hues of rust and dead leaves, glitter in all their radiance greenish golds, yellow ambers, orpiments, raw ochres, chromiums, March oranges!

O dull and gleaming smoked fish, when I contemplate your coat of mail, I recall the paintings of Rembrandt, I see again his superb heads, his sun-drenched flesh, his sparkling gems on black velvet, I see again his rays of light in the night, his trails of gold dust in the shadows, his sunbursts under black arches!

"The Dubois Family" (*La Famille Dubois*): *Saynètes et Monologues*, first series (1877).

As in several other monologues, the scene is a dreary section on the right bank of Paris.

Veloutine was a commercial cosmetic, made of rice powder treated with bismuth. *Acajou* means "mahogany," which means she is also *du bois*, "of wood."

The assessor of sales tax (*jaugeur des droits réunis*) is Cros's invention.

"The Rue Beaubourg Affair" (*L'Affaire de la rue Beaubourg*): *Saynètes et Monologues*, first series (1877).

The rue Beaubourg is an old street in Paris, running through the 3rd and 4th arrondissements. Cros probably chose it for its lack of beauty or interest; it returns in several of the monologues.

"A Man for Amanda" (*L'amant d'Amanda*) is a particularly insipid song by Emile Carré and Victor Robillard, popularized by the comic singer Libert (Xavier Marie Alphonse Libermann), who specialized in portraying dandies. The song was very popular, and Carré came to wish he had never written it.

"The Trip to (Dot Dot Dot)" (*Le Voyage à Trois-Étoiles*): *Saynètes et Monologues*, second series (1877), published as a chapbook in 1883.

"The Bilboquet" (*Le Bilboquet*): First published as a short story in *La Renaissance littéraire et artistique*, September 1873; then in *Étrennes de Parnasse pour 1874;* and was then rewritten as a monologue for *Saynètes et Monologues*, second series (1877).

The bilboquet is a toy consisting of a spiked stick and a ball, the object being to catch the ball on the spike.

"The Maid" (*La Bonne*): *Saynètes et Monologues*, second series (1877).

This is not only the only monologue Cros wrote for a woman, but the only one he designated as a "sketch" (*saynète*). Jeanne Samary was, at one time, Manet's model and paramour. Manet was a close friend of Cros; he illustrated Cros's long poem *Le Fleuve* ("The River"), and loaned paintings for Cros's experiments with color photography.

"The Capitalist" (*Le Capitaliste*): *Saynètes et Monologues*, third series (1878).

1878 was a year marked by unbridled and ill-advised financial speculation in France, especially in the proposed Panama Canal, which ended in failure and scandal.

The Yenisei, I am told, is one of the principal rivers in Siberia.

"The Fencing Master" (*Le Maître d'armes*): *Saynètes et Monologues*, third series (1878).

As a member of the Comédie-Française, Coquelin was no doubt proficient in stage combat, and this gave him a chance to brandish a foil. A film of his brother fencing is still extant.

Cros here uses a number of jokey names, a practice that later became a staple for Allais and other comic writers. Tafta-Gomez is *taffeta gommé*, sticking plaster. The Marquis des Plates-Bandes is named after flowerbeds; *marcher sur les plates-bandes* is to encroach on someone's turf. The Baron Van-Dennefles is, perhaps, engaged in selling medlars, *vendant nèfles*.

"In the Past" (*Autrefois*): *Saynètes et Monologues*, fourth series (1878).

Dreher beer is still brewed in Budapest.

The Saint-Martin canal is a long canal in Paris, running through the 10th and 11th arrondissements.

"The Reasonable Man" (*L'Homme raisonnable*): *Saynètes et Monologues*, fourth series (1878).

The nets in Saint-Cloud, rumored to collect suicides and lost possessions, have been celebrated in Parisian folklore since at least the 18th century. There are no nets there, and that hat is lost forever.

"Obsession" (*L'Obsession*): *Saynètes et Monologues*, fifth series (1879); published as a chapbook in 1881.

This monologue was originally attributed to X. and Charles Cros; the identity of X. remains (dare I say?) mysterious, although it may conceal the composer. Coquelin Cadet however, identified him as Hervé, and the tune as "Saltarello." Hervé (Louis-Auguste-Florimond Ronger) was, in fact, the musical director of the Délassements-Comiques, and composed over a hundred operettas, including *Il Signor Saltarello*. As for the Délassements-Comiques, no fewer than six Parisian theaters bore that name from 1785 to 1890. Our obsessive visited the one that operated on the boulevard Saint-Martin from 1872 to 1878.

For the song, I provided a paraphrase that rhymes and fits the tune; here's a more scrupulous translation:

I just lost my poor aunt,
I just put her in her coffin.
She leaves me a small income,
Which lets me wear mourning.

I had an oak box made for her,
So she can move around with ease.
So she won't feel discomfort,
Where there's discomfort there's no pleasure.

"The Man Who Has Traveled" (*L'Homme qui a voyagé*): *Saynètes et Monologues*, fifth series (1879).

Strumpf is German for "stocking." Today, most French audiences would recognize it as a blue elf, a Schtroumpf (in English, Smurf), from the comic strip Peyo created in 1959.

"The Man Who Was a Success" (*L'Homme qui a réussi*): *Saynètes et Monologues*, sixth series (1880).

I've never made pommes soufflées, but I hear they're tricky.

Prince Chikekski obviously has *chic exquis*, exquisite chic.

The Pressoirs du Roy (King's Winepress) was founded by François I, back in the 16th century.

"The Man With His Feet Turned Around" (*L'Homme aux pieds retournés*): *Théâtre de campagne*, sixth series (1880).

In the original, our hero is named Poyé (that is, *ployé*, bent), which he mistakes for *employé* (employee), and changes to De Poyé (*déployé*, deployed).

The White Rabbit, *Le Lapin Blanc*, is fictional, but inspired by such Parisian department stores as *La Levrette d'Or* (The Golden Greyhound).

"The Lost Man" (*L'Homme perdu*): *Théâtre de campagne*, sixth series (1880).

The headquarters of the Paris police was on the rue de Jérusalem at the time.

The uniform of the Académie Française is known as *l'habit vert*: a long black coat trimmed with elaborate green embroidery.

"The Green Day" (*La Journée verte*): *Tout-Paris*, June 6, 1880; *Saynètes et Monologues*, seventh series (1881).

The boulevard Haussman is noted for its trees.

"The Friend of the Family" (*L'Ami de la maison*): *Théâtre de campagne*, seventh series (1881).

"The Clean Man" (*L'Homme propre*): *Théâtre de campagne*, seventh series (1881); published as a chapbook by Ollendorff in 1883, with illustrations by Cabriol. Cabriol (Georges Lorin) was also a poet, and active in the Hydropathes and the Chat Noir.

Plates-bandes, as mentioned earlier, are flowerbeds.

"The Hanged Man" (*Le Pendu*): *Théâtre de campagne*, seventh series (1881).

This monologue invokes three superstitions: the good luck of unlucky love, hangman's rope, and cuckolds. Alphonse Allais and Maurice Mac-Nab, among others, also exploited the comic potential of these traditions.

La Ferté-sous-Jouarre is a commune in the Île-de-France region, long known for its millstones.

Melissa water is made from *Melissa officinalis*, lemon balm.

"The Man Who Made a Discovery" (*L'Homme qui a trouvé*): *Théâtre de campagne*, seventh series (1881).

Vaugirard was originally a commune in the department of the

Seine, and not formally annexed to Paris until 1860. It can now be found in the 15th arrondissement.

Zebras are, for some reason, proverbially fleet in French.

"The Violin" (*Le Violon*): *Théâtre de campagne*, eighth series (1882).

This is the only monologue in regular verse ("The Salt Herring" is decidedly irregular). My translation retains the meter, but reluctantly abandons the rhymes (ababcdcd). Part of its effect is due to the many unexpected rhymes Cros finds for "violin" (*violon*).

"Property" (*La Propriété*): published as a booklet by Ollendorff, 1888.

French lotto is a parlor game, eerily similar to bingo, and more popular in Cros's time than ours. The numbers were often given facetious names: 11 was "my uncle's two legs," 22 "the two saucepans," 33 "the two hunchbacks," etc. Despite the reference here, there were no triple numbers.

Macouba tobacco comes from Martinique; M. Dubois flavors his with the Tonka bean, from the guaiac tree. The traditional Epiphany cake (*la galette des rois*) includes a small ceramic figure, known as the *fève* (bean); whoever gets it is entitled to wear a paper crown. And France calls itself a republic!

"The Sad Monologue" (*Le monologue triste*) and "Obsession" are taken from *L'art de dire le monologue*, by Coquelin Cadet and Coquelin Aîné, published by Paul Ollendorff in 1884. In his part of the book, Coquelin Cadet discusses several monologues in detail, including these two by Cros. As the astute reader will notice, Coquelin's version of "Obsession" is quite different from the original. Both Coquelin and Félix Galipaux recorded "The Salt Herring" (Coquelin in 1902, Galipaux in 1906). I haven't been able to hear Coquelin's recording, but Galipaux's follows Coquelin's directions closely.

"The Death of Charles Cros" (*La Mort de Charles Cros*): *Le Chat Noir*, August 18, 1888.

Victor Meunier, militant socialist and scientific journalist, contributed to many papers, including the *Rappel*. His article, *Le Son mis en bouteille par M. Charles Cros* ("Sound Bottled by M. Charles Cros"), actually appeared in 1877, not 1876, in the December 11 issue.

Georges Lorin, also known as Cabriol, was, as mentioned earlier in these notes, a Hydropathe and Chat Noir regular.

The photophone, which transmits sound with a light beam, was officially invented in 1880 by Alexander Graham Bell, who, incidentally, considered it his greatest accomplishment. It proved to be less practical than radio. Cros published his *Principes de Mécanique cérébrale* in 1879.

I assume the postscript targets Pierre Delcourt, who vanished from the masthead after this. I don't know what he did, but I hope he learned his lesson.

"Charles Cros and Mr. Edison" (*Charles Cros et M. Edison*): *Le Chat Noir*, September 14, 1889.

All I've been able to learn about the Abbé Leblanc is that his real name was the Abbé Lenoir. How Orwellian!

Although Allais vouched for the accuracy of his dates, he got one wrong and had to correct it in the next issue (I fixed it here).

MORE GOOD SCAT

NO BILE! Alphonse Allais
DOUBLE OVER Alphonse Allais
THE SQUADRON'S UMBRELLA Alphonse Allais
SELECTED PLAYS OF ALPHONSE ALLAIS Alphonse Allais
HIDDEN GEMS: THE BEST OF *THE PEARL* Anonymous
THE MAN WHO WALKED ON AIR Alain Arias-Misson
TINTIN MEETS THE DRAGON QUEEN Alain Arias-Misson
COMIC BOOK Alain Arias-Misson
THE DETECTIVE WHO DIDN'T HAVE A CLUE Alain Arias-Misson
DANTE'S FOIL & OTHER SPORTING TALES Mark Axelrod
SUPERMAN IN AMERICA & OTHER ABSURD PLAYS Mark Axelrod
WAITING FOR GODEAU Honoré de Balzac
THE ZOMBIE OF GREAT PERU Pierre-Corneille de Blessebois
SWEET AND VICIOUS Suzanne Burns
DISORDERED SOULS Tom Bussmann
REAR WINDOWS Norman Conquest
ANGEL OF EVERYTHING Catherine D'Avis
EROTIC TALES Catherine D'Avis
SACRED SINS John Diamond-Nigh
TODAY IS THE DAY THAT WILL MATTER Debra Di Blasi
POSH: AN EROTICAL NOVEL Stephanie Gatos (aka Steve Katz)
MARCO & IARLAITH Eckhard Gerdes
THE OBSERVATORY Petra Anne Hawk
GUSTAVE'S POCKET DICTIONARY Richard Kostelanetz
WHEN I GROW UP AND OTHER MANTRAS Terri Lloyd
THE NEW PLEASURE & OTHER STORIES Pierre Louÿs
WHAT A LIFE! Lucas & Morrow
MISSING MYSTERIES Derek Pell
HERE LIES MEMORY: A PITTSBURGH NOVEL Doug Rice
CLOCKS Jason E. Rolfe
THE UNKNOWN ADJECTIVE & OTHER STORIES Doug Skinner
THE SNOWMAN THREE DOORS DOWN Doug Skinner
SLEEPYTIME CEMETERY: 40 STORIES Doug Skinner
THE DOUG SKINNER SONGBOOK Doug Skinner
THE DOUG SKINNER DOSSIER Doug Skinner
CROCODILE SMILES Yuriy Tarnawsky
TOURIST: A NOVEL Temenuga Trifonova
THE NEW URGE READER 3 Various
LE SCAT NOIR ENCYCLOPAEDIA Various
OULIPO PORNOBONGO ANTHOLOGY Various
THE STRAW THAT BROKE Tom Whalen
CURIOUS IMPOSSIBILITIES Carla M. Wilson
THREE PLAYS BY D. HARLAN WILSON
VAHAZAR Witkacy